THE TIMES OF LAURA GREY

THE TIMES OF LAURA GREY

JOAN SCHMEICHEL

BOOK 1 IN THE LAURA GREY SERIES

Book design by heatherleeshaw.businesscatalyst.com
Cover art: Portrait of María, 1972 by Antonio López Gárcia
Printed in the United States of America.

This book is dedicated to my mother,
whose strength and good humor kept the light
burning through the dark nights.

During the 1930s the Great Depression hung like a dark cloud over the country. Yet for a young girl it was just a part of life.

The important things were school with its good days and bad days and summers that were too short and winters that were too long.

Everybody knows a smack is a kiss,
for goodness sake.

1

THE COLD, WINDY corner is deserted except for a rumpled scarecrow that looks like it blew in from the fields beyond. The scarecrow is me, skinny Laura Grey. Frizzy dishwater hair, pointy nose, and arms and legs like four bent sticks. I'm twelve years old and I'm freezing to death. And if the bus doesn't come by the time I count to one hundred, I'm going home.

It's a lie. I'm not going home. I'm going to the City Library. On Sunday afternoons that's what I do. I sit on the floor by the radiator and read until closing time at five o'clock. I'd take books home with me but I can't unless I have a library card which I don't and I can't get one unless I live in the city which I don't.

We used to live in the city. Before my father lost his job. He didn't lose it exactly, like you lose a handkerchief, but he lost it just the same or he wouldn't be out looking for it all the time. My mother cleans houses, other people's, not ours. We don't have any money. Nobody has any money, for goodness sake, it's 1935. Everybody says it's the Depression. That's not a hole in the ground or anything, it's just a lot of people out of work.

I guess I sound grouchy. It's that awful Christmas party at school. On Friday we drew names for gifts. I drew Rosemary's name! The most popular girl in sixth grade, and the nicest. I can't even hate her. And I'm freezing because the bus won't come.

The bus must have heard me because it waddles down the road and puffs to a stop in front of me. I climb on board and drop my pennies in the glass box. I sit behind the driver where the heat is. It travels up my snow pants and warms my backsides.

I finish *Anne of Green Gables*, just as the library's closing bell sounds. Anne's picture shows she's a bit skinny. Maybe skinny's all right. Maybe skinny's better than Mrs. Praeter, my teacher, who's round and gray like a pigeon.

I shove my skirt back inside my snow pants. My mother says it's to invite pneumonia to let the wind blow up your skirts. I don't think you invite pneumonia. I think it just comes. But if it blows up your skirts, every girl in my class would have it.

I tuck my skirt in because my mother gets after me enough already, usually over my grades. Mrs. Praeter says my mind wanders.

9

It doesn't really go places, like to Africa, it just doesn't pay attention.

I pull on my old socks for mittens and tiptoe down the stairs. One time when I was leaving, my bus money dropped through a hole in my pocket. It clanged on every step. The librarian pointed to the silence sign on her desk. But even without the sign you'd be quiet because the library is like a church, all white with high ceilings. Like the Presbyterian Church with the steeple on top not like Reverend Walls' church in the boarded up store where he stands up front with his three fingers missing praising the Lord and singing about bringing in the sheaves. Somebody said he was a missionary in China. Maybe the Chinese know what a sheave is. I don't.

The library must have been a bank once because it says First City Bank in stone over the door. I don't know if there was ever a second or third. Anyway, I make it safely out the door.

My bus waits on the corner with gray smoke blowing out its tail. That means the heater's on. I head for my favorite seat right on top of it, but somebody got there first so I settle in as close as I can.

It's a windy ten miles home with the bus rocking and bucking across the open road. I hang on to my seat until I see the lights of Zancowski's grocery store, one of the few places in Oakwood Subdivision with electricity. This is where I get off.

Oakwood Subdivision where I live sits in open fields in Michigan, one of the coldest states in the forty eight. The houses are scattered every which way like somebody kicked them and they stuck where they landed. Oakwood doesn't come with city things like electricity and indoor toilets. We have a well to pump water but our toilet is out back. My mother says a job is everything

11

in Oakwood. I wouldn't know. We don't have one.

It's pitch dark now except for tiny specks of light marking some of the houses. I'm anxious to see if ours is one of them. Light means somebody's home and a fire burns in the black iron stove.

Most days I build the fire. A layer of paper, a little coal, a few drops of kerosene from the red can outside the kitchen door, a match, then I slam the door shut to keep the flames inside. Fire is a terrible thing in the country where there's not a lot of water around to put it out. Often at night I hear sirens calling out the volunteers and know somebody's been chased outside in the snow.

Tonight everybody's home for dinner, even my mother. Well, not my father, who's on the road. Everybody else is Edward, who's eighteen, tall, thin, serious and a senior in high school. Thomas is fifteen, wears a big grin, is not serious, and wants to quit ninth grade three days out of five. Elizabeth is sixteen, in eleventh grade, has blazing red hair and sometimes a temper to match.

Edward and Thomas help Gimpy McGee, who lives down by the swamp, deliver packaged coal and cans of kerosene to the neighborhood. Gimpy's mostly respectable, though some people say he steals the coal from the coal yard. Elizabeth takes care of the Wadkins' kids after school. Sometimes I watch Violet Willie whose eyes go two ways and whose brain isn't as big as she is, her mother says. I've been watching over Violet since I was seven and she was ten.

Somebody winds up the old victrola and Straus, one of my mother's only records, is playing. This means dinner's ready. We sit down and everybody talks. Except me. I like to listen.

Thomas starts with Old Mrs. Lockgaar, one of Gimpy's customers. Old Mrs. Lockgaar keeps chickens that fly the coop all the time.

Thomas chases after them for her. He calls it round-up time. Old Mrs. Lockgaar is good to us, sometimes sending a chicken over for our dinner.

I see Old Mrs. Lockgaar every morning on my way to school. That's because she's always outside either sweeping snow off her steps or chasing her chickens. You'd think she'd stay inside where it's warm. I know I would.

The talk at the dinner table winds down and I climb the steps that poke out of a hole in the ceiling. They lead to the attic where Elizabeth and I sleep at one end and Edward and Thomas sleep at the other. Our house is mostly one room with a kitchen on the backside and an attic on top. Behind the kitchen a ways is the toilet. It's in a small house all by itself. In summer it's not too bad but in winter I wish it had a stove.

2

IN THE MORNING I pass Old Mrs. Lockgaar's house on my way to the creek that wanders through the fields. It loops around near the school. I usually drop inside and slide on the ice for the mile or so it takes to get there. This keeps the wind off of me.

This morning there is no wind, so the creek doesn't help much. It's especially cold, too, the kind of cold that makes the snow squeak and glues the insides of your nose together. I'm glad when I reach the school.

Red Ridge School, as it's called for no reason at all as there isn't a ridge in sight, looks like a brick shoebox. Everybody from kindergarten through twelfth grade goes there. It's square in the middle of open fields except for a gray house nearby. A long dirt road leads away from the school and winds up at Oakwood Road. At Oakwood is a feed store, the Red Deer Tavern and the boarded up store front where Reverend Walls preaches. There used to be a gas station but now it's mostly a hole in the ground. This is the town of Red Ridge.

My classroom, sixth grade, is down the hall on the first floor. A coat rack stands outside the door for jackets and lunches. My lunch is in a clean, white bag today. Once I had to use an onion sack. That was terrible. I keep a sharp eye out for good bags now.

Mrs. Praeter hasn't arrived yet. You can tell by the noise inside the classroom. When I open the door, everybody stops talking but they start right up again when they see it's only me.

Sixth grade is a square room with windows on one side and Mrs. Praeter's desk and a long blackboard up front. Rows of wood and metal desks run up and down the middle. They're screwed to the floor so they don't get moved by accident. A bookcase stands against the back wall and a Christmas tree is right beside it. Paper chains and snowflakes decorate the tree. Christmas always brightens the room.

Rosemary waves to me. She waves to everybody. I wave back before heading to my seat. Heidi, who sits next to Rosemary, doesn't wave. Rosemary is nice and Heidi is mean. They're best friends.

The room buzzes with talk. Except for Florence Cox, who doesn't talk to anybody. She just sits hunched over by the window. Every day she stares outside.

I guess if there's one person in the whole world worse off than I am it's Florence. She has lank hair that lets both ears peek out and a whispery voice so low that nobody can hear what she says even if they wanted to which they don't.

Florence lives in that old house by the school. It looks like it had a porch once but it's gone. All that's left are some broken boards that bang against one another in the wind. Florence has a bunch of younger brothers and sisters and her mother screams at them every recess and lunch hour.

I feel sorry for Florence and sometimes want to talk to her. I don't try very hard though and feel guilty about it. It seems some girls have everything and some have nothing. Rosemary, for example, has everything and Florence nothing. I guess I have almost nothing.

Mrs. Praeter comes in and announces an arithmetic drill. Why does arithmetic have to be first thing in the morning? First thing in the morning is too early for anything, especially arithmetic. Besides, I hate drills. I'm the last one standing and the first one sitting down. I can't think on my feet. As soon as I stand up, my brains sink to my toes.

The morning passes slowly as I wait for lunchtime. Finally the bell rings and I get my lunch from where it rests on top of the coat rack. I take my new bag to the Kindergarten Room, where those who don't go home eat lunch. Mrs. Rostenveld, the kindergarten teacher, supervises lunch time. She hates crumbs. I mean really hates them. You better not leave one crumb any place. If you do, you have to eat off the floor. I never have but I know it's true.

After lunch, everybody goes outside. That's the rule.

"Fox and geese!"

"Fox and geese!"

Everybody wants to play the game where a fox chases a bunch of geese around a wagon wheel tramped out in the snow.

As I wander across the playground, hoping Rosemary will ask me to play, a voice yells at me. It's a voice that you know comes with red hair and freckles. Sheldon! Lately every time I'm around, he throws snowballs or something. I hate it. He's big and clumsy and even dumber in school than I am. He never comes to school during planting season and misses a lot during harvest. Sheldon lives on a farm, like almost everybody else around here.

"Duck, Leery!" he yells, calling me by that nickname he made up out of nothing at all. "Here I come."

Before I can move, he's leap-frogging over my back, shoving me into the snow. I spit slush from my mouth and screech at him.

"Sheldon, you're a hoodlum!" My mother's favorite word, "A dim witted imbecile," Elizabeth's favorite and "A snip nose!" my own. "I hate you!" For good measure, I add, "Someday I'm going to give you a smack!"

Everybody stops what they're doing. They stare. They shriek with laughter. Sheldon claps his hands and jumps up and down.

"Leery, Leery!" he calls, "Someday I'll give YOU a smack, like this." He puckers up.

My face burns. I swallow hard. What have I done? Rosemary comes up and pats my shoulder but the laughter continues until the ringing bell finally lets me escape.

The rest of the day every time the teacher's back is turned, one of the boys puckers up and points to Sheldon. What if he tries to catch me? Can I outrun him? I wonder for the millionth time how I could have been so stupid. Everybody knows a smack is a kiss, for goodness sake.

The final bell rings and I jump up. I can be out the door before Sheldon moves. I can be halfway home before he gets his boots on.

I peek out the front door. Nobody is around. I sneak outside. Sheldon leaps from behind the school. He's followed by a cluster of rowdy boys.

"Pucker up, Leery."

"Cheeks like roses, nose like hoses."

I run as fast as I can. I know Sheldon's lumbering behind me. I imagine I can hear his laughter. I run half way home before chancing a look. There's no one back there but Ellen Allen who's a year younger than I am and lives in the subdivision.

Ellen and I play together sometimes. Not too often because she can't come to my house and I can't go to hers when her father's home. That's because Ellen's father hates my mother since she called him a hoodlum and an animal when he cuffed his wife outside Zancowski's grocery store. My mother says somebody needs to teach Mr. Allen a lesson.

I wait for Ellen to catch up. She wants me to come over. Her pa isn't home, she says. Ellen and I usually play most beautiful where Ellen gets to be the most beautiful girl in the world and I get to be anybody else. Today she wants me to come over and play paper dolls.

We follow a path that branches off from the creek to Ellen's back porch. The porch is hung with gray rags stiffening in the cold, but Ellen's kitchen is warm and Mrs. Allen friendly. She grins at us now from her post by the oil stove where she's keeping a cup of tea warm.

Mrs. Allen's a tall, stooped woman with bare legs, bulging veins and a missing tooth in front. None of this seems to bother her much. I like Mrs. Allen and guess I could sometimes be most beautiful if we were to ever play together.

I stay longer at Ellen's house than I should. It's dark when I walk up the front path to our door. Our house is a tar-paper covered place about the size of the sixth grade classroom. A small room sticking out the backside holds a kerosene cook stove, an icebox and a sink with pump for water. In summer roses climb the walls of the house but in winter the roses look like hair that needs combing. Like mine, I guess. My hair looks like it does for probably the same reason I'm so skinny and my eyes are neither blue nor green. It's because I'm the youngest in the family. Thomas says I got all the leftover parts.

I pound on the door. An angry Thomas lets me in, demanding to know where I've been. "Elizabeth and I have been hollering all over for you and Edward's on his way back to school."

This is serious. My brothers stick together since the Klewicki boys caught Thomas behind Gimpy's place and gave him a licking because he saw Darrell Klewicki peeing in one of Gimpy's kerosene cans. Gimpy's orange haired girlfriend chased them off. Darrell and Clarence Klewicki are the meanest boys in the whole county. They live down by the swamp not too far from Gimpy McGee. One Eye Klewicki, their father, is as mean as they are. My mother says One Eye's a bum by habit and a chicken thief by inclination. He doesn't really have only one eye, only one that he can see out of. Some say he lost it in the war and some say he lost it when his wife hit him on the head with a frying pan when she left him. We didn't tell our mother about the Klewicki boys getting after Thomas. She would have marched over and given the Klewickis a piece of her mind. We try to avoid that.

I promise to come straight home from school—and wash everybody's socks for a week. I guess it could have been worse. The good thing is I go to bed and forget about Sheldon.

3

THIS MORNING I'm not noticing the cold. That's because I'm thinking about Sheldon and the smack. That's what came into my mind the minute I woke up this morning. It takes up so much room that I don't have any left over to think about the cold. I wonder again how I could have been so dumb.

Maybe everybody forgot about it. There are lots of other things to think about this close to Christmas. I cheer myself with that thought. Then, thinking of Christmas, I'm reminded of whose name I drew.

The first bell is ringing as I reach the school. I hurry inside and rush down the hall.

Sheldon sneaks up behind me as I hang my things on the coat rack. "I sure would like my smack, Leery," he whispers before running off. I could smack somebody.

"Pucker up, Laura," Fat Eddie whispers the minute I step inside the classroom door. He points at Sheldon. My face turns red and I take my seat.

Nobody forgets. Nobody forgets for the whole week. Sheldon teases me and the other boys egg him on. By the end of the week I'm almost used to it. I guess you can get used to anything.

Now it's Thursday night and the Christmas party is the next day. I sit at the table and stare at Rosemary's gift. A handkerchief case! Who ever heard of such a thing? It was my mother's idea and she's probably the only person in the entire world who knows what it is. Why did I let her talk me into it? Because I had nothing else, that's why.

"I'll have to tell her what it is," I announce to Edward who sits next to me doing his homework. "She'll never in a million years know if I don't tell her. Nobody knows what a handkerchief case is."

I stare at the blue satin case on the table in front of me. I admire the pink ribbons I sewed on the side and the pink flowers I embroidered in all the corners. I have to admit that the handkerchief case cut from my mother's old slip is pretty. In the light of the kerosene lamp it gleams like precious silver.

"I'll still have to tell her what it is," I continue as I apply a Santa Claus sticker to the now wrapped package.

"Are you talking to me?" Edward asks after I've finished.

I head for the steps to the attic. "No, I was talking to Santa Claus."

"Oh." He goes back to work.

Edward's like that sometimes. It never bothers me. I have other things to think about, like my clothes.

I climb the attic steps and sit on the bed. Wrapped in the quilt I think about self improvement. My hair is the worst. Maybe I can roll it up like Elizabeth. Maybe I can pull it back. Maybe I can shave it off. Forget the hair. Maybe I can borrow Elizabeth's skirt. What if I roll it at the waist and borrow one of her sweaters to hide the roll? Elizabeth's navy sweater is perfect except for a hole in the sleeve. I can mend that.

"Elizabeth," I call out, heading back down the steps when she comes in.

Extracting vows of cleanliness and obedience, Elizabeth loans me her skirt and sweater. I mend the sweater with white thread and dab a little ink on it.

After dinner I climb back to the attic. It's a cozy place, filled with bright feather beds and quilts. All it needs is heat. I snuggle down.

Only three days before Sunday. Maybe I can find another book like *Anne of Green Gables*. I put myself to sleep with that thought.

4

FRIDAY MORNING I open my eyes to a soft white blanket on the bed, a dusting of snow that came in through the cracks in the wall.

"I could be buried until spring," I call to Elizabeth who is already up and dressed.

"Just be sure to shake the quilts when you get up," she tells me. Elizabeth never seems to get cold. Maybe she stays warm because of her red hair. I blush, thinking about Sheldon's red hair.

If I stay in bed, I can skip the party. But my mother would probably find out I stayed home from school. I get up and dress in Elizabeth's clothes. The skirt hangs on my bones. I want to cry but the tears will freeze on my face. I slip into a rumpled dress and cover it with Elizabeth's sweater.

When I climb downstairs, everyone is gone. Oatmeal and stewed prunes wait for me. I gulp them down before leaving.

As I walk by Old Mrs. Lockgaar's, she beckons me over. Today she's wrapped in dead Old Mr. Lockgaar's giant sweater. Both pockets bulge.

She begins by saying as she heard how I like to read and how she could never see much sense in it herself and I was welcome to these if I wanted them. She finishes with a little cackle and pulls two thick books from her pockets.

I'm so surprised by the length of the speech—I had never heard Old Mrs. Lockgaar say more than half a dozen words—that it takes a minute to realize what I hold in my hands. Two books by Charles Dickens! I can hardly believe my eyes. I surprise Old Mrs.

Lockgaar and myself with a yell so loud that the old woman claims her chickens won't lay for a month. She pokes me with a bony finger and tells me to leave the books and pick them up after school, that I better get going.

I take her advice and hurry off, trying not to think of Rosemary's present or Sheldon's smacks.

At school everything and everybody sparkles. The students are dressed in Sunday bests. The boys wear corduroy knickers and sleeveless sweaters. They sport clean fingernails and slicked-back hair. The girls are fluffed in dresses and party jumpers.

When I see Rosemary, I gasp. She wears pink velvet with big puffy sleeves and a wide ribbon at the waist. Her blond hair, tied with pink ribbons, hangs in giant sausages, only much prettier of course.

Everybody crowds around her, everybody except Florence, that is, who sits in her usual seat wearing her usual brown jumper and dirty white blouse. I'm glad I have Elizabeth's sweater on. I can't hope to look like Rosemary but I feel like a better Laura.

I slide my gift under the tree and take my seat. Nobody teases me, not one person. I glance at Sheldon. He's busy slicking down his hair with one big freckled hand and examining the cracked plaster on the ceiling while whistling "Deck the Halls."

He looks sillier than usual, in a green sleeveless sweater that must have belonged to his father from the way it hangs on him.

The day drags on. I'm not looking forward to the party but I want to start my new books. Sheldon continues to ignore me and the smack seems forgotten. Everybody is too busy giggling and passing notes to think about me.

Finally three o'clock arrives. Desks are cleared. Mrs. Praeter selects a few students to set up for the party. The rest may go to the lavatory. I'm surprised to be chosen to help. It has never happened before. Mrs. Praeter asks me to distribute her gift to the students: a red paper Christmas stocking with a striped candy cane inside. While I do this, she brings in a steaming pot of hot cocoa.

In a minute the rest of the class returns, excited and noisy:

"Quit shoving!"

"You'll muss my dress."

"Get off my shoes!"

Mrs. Praeter hushes everybody by writing "Silent Night" on the blackboard. She begins to sing "Deck the Halls" and we join in with gusto, especially the fa, la, la part. Next, Rosemary plays Santa Claus and passes out the gifts. Mrs. Praeter has the most gifts, with everybody trying to give her something. I made a pine cone snowman to hang on her tree. The next biggest pile is on Rosemary's desk. But everybody has at least one gift, plus Mrs. Praeter's stocking.

Mrs. Praeter fills our milk cups from her steaming pot, then says "Merry Christmas."

That's the signal. Wrapping paper flies amidst squeals and shrieks, yells and whoops and some groans.

I'm in dread, too nervous to open the brown paper package on my own desk. I watch Rosemary. She has my gift in her hands. She unties the string. I hold my breath. I squeeze down in my seat.

"How pretty," her voice comes across the room. "A handkerchief case. And I have a new handkerchief right here to put in it. Thank you, Laura."

Rosemary is looking right at me. I can hardly believe my ears! She knows what it is! She even likes it, unless she's just being nice. But it doesn't matter. She knows what it is. I don't have to tell her.

Now I can turn to my own gift. As I do, a small, fretful voice floats down from somewhere around my left ear. It's Florence and she's saying something too painful to speak aloud.

"Leery," she whispers. "Ain't but one piece gone n' yer so foxy, you kin fer certain make another." The voice stops a moment then continues on before fading away altogether. "It's all I had."

I look at my Christmas gift. It's a used puzzle with, as Florence said, one piece missing. I feel a sharp stab of disappointment, and a sadness. Christmas is never as good as it's supposed to be. Then I remember Florence. Too late. She's already gone back to her seat.

I sort through my desk to find pencil and paper. "I hate stupid, boring puzzles," I write. "This one will be twice as hard and twice the fun." I start to sign it "Laura" but change my mind and write "Your friend Laura." I pass the note over to Florence and watch her face brighten as she reads it.

The puzzle is the three Wise Men, now mostly only two I guess. I blink and turn to my hot cocoa. Suddenly a thought comes to me. Foxy? Nobody has ever called me foxy before. I feel a smile building on my face. I look at the puzzle again then carefully put the lid back on.

The party ends. We clear our desks of all signs of Christmas. I fill the brown paper bag I brought from home with Mrs. Praeter's Christmas stocking and my new puzzle.

In the hall I pull on snow pants and galoshes and don't complain once, not even when I see snow swirling outside the school door. I tuck my paper bag inside my coat and leave.

Cold air and wet flakes smack into my face. I'm glad my Christmas things are hidden away. Icy crystals settle on my eyelids and blur the road in front of me. I clutch the bag tight to my chest.

As I pass by Florence's house, I hear a voice whistling through the snow.

"Leery!"

"Leery, wait!"

My heart begins to thump. I want to run. I grit my teeth and duck my head to keep the snow out of my eyes. I watch the road where drifting snow is beginning to hide the ditch alongside.

Suddenly I feel a tug on my arm. Gentle as it is, I jump and begin to shake. A blurred face and frosted red hair shoves its way right in front of my nose. The smack is coming. I know it. I should have run, after all.

"Merry Christmas, Leery!" Sheldon's voice sounds hoarse. He pushes a small, white bag into my hand then disappears in the next gust of snow.

I look fearfully at the bag. I hold it away from me. Is it a firecracker ready to go off? I shake it. Nothing happens. I turn my back to the wind. Shielding the bag from the snow, I look inside.

A half dozen taffy candy kisses rest underneath a folded note. "Kisses for Laura," the note says.

My cheeks feel hot instead of cold and my eyes are wet. I brush the snow off my coat and unbutton it. Sheldon's gift goes in the bag, right beside my puzzle from Florence and the Christmas stocking from Mrs. Praeter.

First I'll go to Old Mrs. Lockgaar's. Then I'll go home and build a fire. Then I'll sit in the blue chair by the stove with my Christmas gifts around me.

I laugh and kick the snow into puffy clouds. They dance around my face and don't feel cold at all.

*Don't you think a new year should
bring something new?*

5

CHRISTMAS HAS COME and gone
and now it's back to school. It was a good
Christmas, though. I got white figure skates
that my mother brought home from work,
the lady not wanting them anymore. I also
got a new pair of snow pants from welfare.
Edward gave me barrettes for my hair and
Elizabeth gave me a scarf she knitted herself.
Thomas gave me a pencil and a big pad of
paper. He said I like to read so much that I
should write my own stories so I don't ever
run out. Thomas is silly.

Elizabeth and I went to Reverend Walls'
to see the New Year come in. There was

nothing to see. We sat around with some mostly old people until midnight when Mrs. Walls served apple cake and cider. The cider tasted funny but the cake was really good. Everybody left right after the cake.

This morning the snow is especially deep. After I climb out of the creek I scuff my galoshes all the way to the front door of the school. When I look back I see a trail that looks like two giant worms are following me. Snow is good for more than fox and geese, I guess.

I open the door to the school and a blast of warm air invites me inside. With the Christmas decorations gone, the school looks exactly the same in 1936 as it did in 1935. It even smells the same, of chalk dust and wet wool, a smell that includes my own snow-covered coat, which I hang on the rack outside the sixth grade classroom.

Don't you think a new year should bring something new? Take me, I'm still the same.

The school's the same. The books from Old Mrs. Lockgaar are new, though, at least to me. The books are funny. Not funny to laugh at but funny in that they don't make sense. Take *A Tale of Two Cities*, where this man says it's a better thing that he gets his head chopped off. He should keep his head. It's a story, after all. If I were a story, I'd give my father a job and us indoor plumbing. See what I mean?

"Good morning, class."

I make it to my seat just as Mrs. Praeter, comes into the classroom.

"Good morning, Mrs. Praeter," we sing out.

"Class," Mrs. Praeter continues: "I want you to welcome a new student to our school."

New? My ears perk up.

Mrs. Praeter turns to the door. "Eldora, come in, please."

Something comes through the door. It's wearing a ruffled dress and a hair bow that looks like a cluster of butterflies. Eldora, our new classmate, is a creature of arms and legs skinnier than mine, straight, dark hair no longer than her ears, round silver glasses and freckles like red measles running up and down her nose.

She takes a stance behind and to the side of Mrs. Praeter.

"Class," Mrs. Praeter introduces her. "This is Eldora Francis Fairfield."

Eldora sticks out her tongue and rolls her eyes. "She comes to us from Cincinnati, Ohio." Eldora pushes her nostrils up with two fingers and pulls her eyes down with the other two. "Her father is the new owner of the Red Deer Tavern." With this, Eldora carries a make-believe glass to her lips, gulps it down, wipes her mouth with the back of her hand and looks happy but cross-eyed. "I know you will make her feel at home," finishes Mrs. Praeter,

The class, wide-eyed, mumbles hello. Eldora walks surely and smugly to a seat in the front row, the vacancy arranged by God, I think.

It's soon clear that Eldora knows everything. Mrs. Praeter beams and Heidi grimaces as Eldora answers every question. At recess, to the horror of the girls and the red faces of the boys, Eldora tells embarrassing things about animals. She refuses to play fox-and-geese, everybody's favorite winter game.

Nobody knows what to think of her. Except me. I know enough to stay away from her.

Rosemary, always friendly to everybody, gives her a welcoming pat and a warm smile. In response, Eldora scratches her belly like a monkey. When Heidi, who thinks she's the smartest girl in class but is only the most stuck-up, brags about her father's feed store, Eldora neighs like a horse. The boys make faces behind Eldora's back but hang on every word.

6

A WHOLE WEEK PASSES and Eldora is still the same. In class she reads aloud better than Mrs. Praeter and is the last one standing in arithmetic drills. During recess she thinks up games to play and crazy things to do. At times she ignores everybody.

One day after a heavy snowfall and a rejection of fox-and-geese in a nasty way, Eldora walks to the corner of the school and starts a snowman. It's going to be a giant. I watch with interest as she works on it all morning recess and during lunch hour. From my place by the door I try not to let her catch me watching, but I cast gleeful looks as she packs snow in one place and carves it out in another. I am barely able to keep from laughing out loud. It's Mrs. Praeter, for goodness sake, pigeon shape and all.

Eldora stands back to admire her work. She cocks her head right and left. Satisfied, she heads straight for me. What have I done? Go away, I want to yell. I see Florence and decide to be friendly. But Florence is hard at work cleaning her nose and wiping it on her jacket. I walk away, feeling guilty. I always feel guilty about Florence.

Eldora's almost over to me. I turn to the door, like there's something interesting written on it.

"How come you have your nose stuck in the door?" Her voice hits the back of my head like a hammer. "You look like a dog at a meat market. Come help me with my snowman," she orders.

My scalp prickles and my hands feel sweaty. I see red spots before my eyes. What business is it of this strange girl from Ohio where I stick my nose? I yell I'd rather be a dog than a monkey because that's what she is, a chicken-headed monkey.

Is this me? Me, who never calls attention to herself?

My vision clears and I see Eldora standing with her mouth open and the freckles on her nose bouncing around like drops of water on a hot stove.

"Besides," I add. "It's not a snowman; it's a snow-woman."

Eldora's expression turns from astonishment to delight. Her glasses fall to the tip of her nose. She jumps up and down and flaps her arms. She pokes me with her elbow. Before I can stop myself, I poke her back. Eldora clucks like a chicken. For some reason I bark like dog.

The next thing I know, Eldora's running off flapping her arms like a chicken and I'm chasing her barking like a dog. We run smack in the middle of fox-and-geese. The players kick snow as us and we kick back. By the time the bell rings, everybody's covered with snow. But everybody's laughing! For goodness sake.

All the way home, with the wind and snow practically blowing me off my feet, I think about Eldora. What a funny girl she is. I want to tell somebody about her. But nobody's home. The house is dark and vacant.

The next morning when I arrive at school, Eldora's waiting for me. "We'll track rabbits today," she says, her twitching freckles making her look like a rabbit. "I study animal tracks," she adds, as if to make sense of anything.

Surprised by this sharing of information, I try to think of something interesting to say about myself. I can't think of anything. Eldora waits a minute, then gives my scarf a jerk and walks off.

At recess we tramp around the school looking for tracks long since smeared by boots from kindergarten through twelfth grade.

Eldora won't give up though. She insists we try during lunch recess.

Eldora's father comes by and takes her to the Red Deer for lunch. I take my lunch to the kindergarten room.

After lunch Eldora leads me to a nearby field filled with snowdrifts as tall as we are. We make a nest in the snow. With a gleeful laugh, she pulls a thermos bottle out of her fur muff. The sweet smell of cocoa fills the air. We take turns sipping the hot, syrupy liquid.

Eldora's a real person, I decide right then and there. Not like me, for goodness sake; who would want to be like me. But she's a real person in some other strange way, a person who wears party dresses to play in and fur bonnets and muffs to dig in the snow.

"My father buys all my clothes," Eldora says suddenly, like she knows what I'm thinking. "He orders everything from the Montgomery Ward catalog: dresses, coats, galoshes, hair bows, even underwear. You should see my underpants. They have the days of the week embroidered on them." She giggles. "Sometimes I wear a Thursday on Sunday." She takes a sip of cocoa and hands the cup to me.

Amazing. Eldora's not afraid to talk about anything, even underwear.

7

ONE SATURDAY in March I decide to go to Eldora's. For weeks she's been after me to come, saying she had something to show me. But her house is way on the other side of the school, at least two miles from mine and in winter two miles is like a million. This morning, though, a streak of sunlight coming through the window makes the day seem almost warm.

Before leaving for Eldora's, I stop by Mrs. Willie's to see if Violet needs watching. I wait awhile for Mrs. Willie to get to the door. Mrs. Willie is fat, fatter than almost anybody, I guess. I sometimes think if she grew straight

up instead of sideways, she'd be really tall.
She answers my knock, telling me Violet
doesn't need watching today.

I head for Eldora's, the same way I go to
school, by following the creek. I climb out
at the school and head for Oakwood Road.
Eldora said to take Oakwood for about a mile
and then go left on Hollow Road for another
half mile. If I angle through the woods off
Oakwood, I bet I can cut the distance almost
in half.

The woods looks inviting. Sunlight
sparkles on the snow and diamond trickles of
water slide down dark tree trunks. I decide to
try the shortcut.

Animal tracks keep me company as I
walk. The deeper into the woods I go, the
more tracks I see. Deer, rabbit, dog, all mixed
together so I can't tell one from the other.
Suddenly I come across tracks I do recognize,
those of man-size boots. They circle in from

where the Klewickis live. I shiver, thinking of the Klewicki boys.

All at once it seems I've been in the woods a long time. I stop to listen. The wind has picked up. It whistles through small branches overhead and creates shadowy fingers on the snow. The woods aren't friendly any more.

My mother feels strongly about the woods. My mother feels strongly about a lot of things: school, my grades, my messy hair, Mr. Allen who knocks his wife around, the Klewicki boys who knock my brothers around. I try not to get her to feeling too strongly about me. I won't tell her about taking the shortcut through the woods.

But what if she finds out when they bring her the sad news of her daughter? Shut up, for goodness sake, I tell myself. I decide to run.

"It's not far," I yell, in case anybody's listening. I feel silly even as I do it. There's nothing to be afraid of. The sun is shining.

The woods are filled with light. I tighten my scarf and pull my hat down.

Running doesn't work too well. Broken branches hiding under the snow grab my feet. They threaten to send me flying. Strange crackling and rustling noises fill my ears. The sounds are mine, I know. Yet I run faster, not sure I believe it. My eyes and nose fill with snow. Blood pounds in my ears. It drowns out everything but the thumping of my heart. I stumble and grab a tree to keep from falling. Gasping and fearful, I try to run even faster.

Suddenly, with a sharp crack, a dead branch snaps under my feet. A jagged end flies up at my face. I scream and cover my eyes. Seconds later I crash into a pile of broken branches and dead leaves hiding under the snow. The sound is deafening to my ears.

As the noise fades away, I lie still, listening. Do I hear something? I stop breathing. I try to squeeze my heart into silence. Yes! There

it is! The sound of running feet! Someone—
or something—is coming!

"Leery! Leery!"

Sheldon! I try to hold back tears of relief.
The tracks must have belonged to him.

"Leery! Are you all right?" He emerges
through the trees, a shotgun in one hand and
an empty gunnysack in the other. "I saw you
running awhile back and wondered." He sets
his sack and gun down. "Is something wrong?
Are you hurt?" He kneels and tries to brush
leaves and twigs from my hair.

I want to die from shame. How can I let
this big, dumb farm boy know I was afraid of
my own feet!

"I got snow in my eyes and up my nose,"
I tell him. "I was following a rabbit, if you
must know, a big, white one," I lie. "And
now you've probably scared him off."

Sheldon looks at me questioningly.
"Well," he finally says, with a smile. "If you
see him again, let me know, will you? I've

been huntin' rabbits all morning and haven't seen a one. We were hopin' for rabbit stew for supper, too."

He picks up my hat and beats the snow off on his arm. "Where you headed? To that dodo Eldora's?" He doesn't wait for an answer. "I'll walk with you, since you seem to see all the rabbits."

"I can find my way," I tell him. "Just give me my hat."

He holds it out. "You can have it for a kiss."

"You're disgusting, Sheldon. I'll never kiss you!"

"You want your hat or don't you?" he asks, tossing it in the air, daring me to catch it.

Sheldon's always after me to kiss him. I can't think of anything worse than kissing a boy, especially Sheldon.

"Leery, Leery, give us a kiss," he teases. "Pucker up and do it like this." He makes a face.

I reach my foot back to kick him. He jumps out of the way and I grab my hat.

He doesn't seem to notice. "Come on. I'll walk you to Eldora's," is all he says.

"You better catch your rabbit dinner instead," I tell him.

"Rabbits are good to eat," he wants me to know.

I shiver, thinking of Peter Rabbit in Sheldon's stew. Then I decide that's not much different than Peter on Eldora's muff.

Sheldon tells me he hunts a lot, especially in winter when work on the farm is slow and he can follow animal tracks in the snow.

"Don't you ever read books?" I ask, curious about this boy who kills rabbits and always wants to kiss me.

"Not unless I have to," he answers. "It's too much work. It's not like tossing hay or working the plow. That's work, too, but it's fun work."

It doesn't sound like fun to me. I don't say it, though. We're at Eldora's house and I head to the back door, avoiding a broken dog house in my path.

"Don't chase any more rabbits today," Sheldon yells as he leaves.

My face burns. I wish I had stayed buried in the leaves.

8

I KNOCK on Eldora's door. A woman dressed in a bathrobe peers out at me. She doesn't say anything, just disappears. I'm wondering what to do next when Eldora comes to the door. "I'll just be a minute," she says, not inviting me in.

I'm disappointed, having hoped for a chance to warm up.

Without so much as a hello, Eldora appears and says: "Follow me." She leads me into the woods behind her house. After a long walk, she stops and points to a giant, fallen tree. Between the tree's trunk and one of its branches sits a spread-out building. I can see where most of the doghouse went.

"Our fort," Eldora proudly tells me. "The minute I saw the tree I knew it was perfect." She climbs on the trunk. "You have to get in from the top," she explains, folding back half the roof.

I follow her up and we drop inside, sliding the roof back in place. I can see that the fort is about the size of two or three doghouses. I hope there are no fleas.

Eldora lights three candles stuck in cans. I can now see a wood floor, a throw rug that looks suspiciously like one of Eldora's coats, and two stools. Books and candle stubs sit on a box in the corner. The room feels warm and cozy. Eldora hands me a cinnamon bun frosted with pocket lint. We sit on the stools, eating and spitting.

"I read books and study animals here," Eldora says, between bites and spits. "Mostly I stay away from the house."

She doesn't say why and I don't ask. People are entitled to say only what they want to, I figure. They shouldn't be pushed into saying more. I know there are a lot of things I never say to anybody.

"What are you going to be?" Eldora asks suddenly. "I want to be a scientist; but if I can't, I may just dig ditches."

"I won't dig ditches," I tell her, knowing that right off. My father dug ditches once and every night he came home with mud up his nose.

"Maybe you'll get married and have lots of babies," Eldora said. "I'm not going to get married, though."

"I wouldn't like washing all those dirty diapers," I tell her. The stories I read don't talk about diapers; they only talk about living happily ever after. I don't think washing dirty diapers is living happily ever after.

"Have you noticed how Heidi's getting all the answers right?" Eldora asks, not interested in marriage talk any more.

I had noticed. "She seems to get smarter every week."

Eldora laughs. "Maybe it's all those oats she's eating." Then she gets serious. "She's cheating. I don't know how yet. What I do know is that she's too dumb to be so smart."

A horn blasts through the woods. I jump up and almost hit my head on the roof. Eldora nods. "It's a boat horn," she explains. "Papa's home for an early dinner."

We lift the roof off and walk back to Eldora's. I take the road home.

9

MONDAY MORNING Mrs. Praeter announces an arithmetic test. Groans and moans, carefully hidden behind raised books, greet her words. "I told you on Friday," she reminds us.

"I think I know what she's doing," Eldora whispers when I pass her desk to sharpen my pencil. "Wait until recess," she says with a smile. It's not a nice smile.

She? Then I remember what Eldora said about Heidi cheating.

Mrs. Praeter collects our test papers, then tells us to line up in the hall before we go outside for recess. Recess will be late today, she explains, because the visiting nurse is here.

I know what that means. The visiting nurse is here to check our heads for lice. She comes every year and pokes through our hair with wooden sticks. Everybody hates it. Lots worse, though, is if she comes to your house and finds somebody sick. She puts a red sign on your door and nobody can go to work. You have to be careful around the visiting nurse.

Anyway, little Petey in fourth grade must have had lice because the day after the visiting nurse was here, he came to school bald.

Eldora never heard of anybody checking for lice. I guess they don't have lice in Cincinnati. I have to tell her what it's all about. She says nobody's going to look into her head and I guess they don't because she hides in the lavatory.

After the visiting nurse is through, we go to recess. I hurry outside to see what Eldora's up to about Heidi. "Watch," she whispers and pulls something from her snow pants.

"Oh, Laura," Eldora calls in a loud voice. "Help me write these answers down." She pretends to scribble on a piece of pink paper for a minute. Then, as the entire sixth-grade watches, she snaps open a pair of bulging pink bloomers covered with arithmetic answers. They flap in the breeze like a flag on the Fourth of July.

"Want to borrow these?" Eldora asks Heidi. "They hold more answers than you can stick in your stockings."

Heidi's eyes pop and her face breaks out in purple blotches. She grabs at the bloomers. They rip down the middle. Half a bloomer sails across the school yard where it settles into a puddle of melting snow. It floats there, a pink blob, until Sheldon walks over and plants a rubber galosh right in the middle of it.

"You're just jealous," Heidi yells at Eldora. "You're just jealous because I beat you." She sticks her tongue out. "And nobody likes you either. You think you're so smart all the time!"

As there's some truth in the last, I look to Eldora to respond. But Heidi's not finished.

"My ma says if your daddy didn't sell sinful whiskey like he does, your ma wouldn't be drunk all the time like she is."

Eldora's freckles stand out against her white face. Her hands clench into fists. "My mama and papa are none of your beeswax, cheater," she tells Heidi coldly. "You're a dumb cheat. Half the time you get the answers wrong anyway."

"Heidi! What a rotten thing to say about Eldora's mother!" I wait for Eldora's sharp tongue to pick up where I left off. But she's silent.

Everybody stands around not knowing what to do until Rosemary mops up the quarrel with smiles and pats and licorice buttons. I take a button, feeling disloyal, but Eldora takes one, too. Then we leave the others and sit on our heels beside a puddle where we send stick boats out to sea. Neither one of us speaks. Eldora licks her lips with a charcoal tongue and shoves her glasses aside to rub a mittened hand across her eyes.

Eldora shouldn't cry! I feel afraid for her and spit out the black button.

"I hate her," whispers Eldora.

"She's just a cheat and a big mouth," I tell her. "Don't let her make you feel bad."

"Not Heidi, she's dumb." Eldora looks up at me. "It's Mama I hate." She wipes her glasses and puts them back on. "I hate them both. Papa's to blame. He should make her stop drinking."

I want to say something comforting, but can think of nothing.

"Papa talks about sending me away to boarding school," Eldora whispers as we head back to the classroom. "Sometimes I wish he would so I didn't have to live with them anymore." Her words make her seem both young and old at the same time.

10

AFTER THAT, I SEE Eldora's mother drunk once. It's a terrible thing to see.

Eldora is usually careful, but one day she invites me in to pick out a book to take home. I had just finished when I see Eldora's eyes fly to the door of her room. She looks away, as though by not looking, what she sees will disappear.

It's Eldora's mother, leaning against the doorway. She's young, I think, lots younger than my mother. It's hard to tell, though, because her long brown hair is matted around her face.

"Home so schoon, Dor?" she says, sounding like her teeth are missing. She weaves back and forth, then slides down the doorjamb, easy-like, as though somebody had pulled the stays from her corset. She shoves her hair aside.

"I shlipped a little," she comments.

Eldora doesn't say anything until her mother pulls herself up and staggers off. "See what I mean," she says.

"I see." There doesn't seem to be anything else to say.

We don't talk about Eldora's mother after that. We talk about the end of the school year and our plans for summer. We talk about expanding the fort, turning it into a real house. Eldora is making a drawing.

With only three weeks of school left, Eldora announces one Friday that she has finished her drawing. If I come in early on Monday and meet her at the creek, she'll show it to me. She knows getting to school early isn't something I usually do.

Monday arrives and I'm waiting at the creek. The morning is warm and sunny so I don't mind waiting. But it seems like I've been waiting a long time. Finally I run to school, not sure what time it is or how late I may be. Maybe Eldora forgot. But I can't imagine Eldora forgetting anything.

When I open the classroom door everybody stops talking, as usual. Only they don't start up again when they see it's only me. I notice that Eldora's desk is empty. Nobody looks at me, except Heidi, who has a funny look on her face. Sheldon is sitting on the window ledge, staring at his shoes. I take my seat.

Finally Rosemary comes over. "The door of the Red Deer was found open Friday night," she says.

Heidi follows, eager to tell: "Constable Martin found Eldora's mother inside. She was hanging from the ceiling light."

My scalp prickles.

"Constable Martin cut her down before she…" Heidi lowers her voice, like she's using dirty words. "…before she killed herself."

I want to slap her. But I feel too sick. I run to the lavatory and lean over the sink, trying to throw up. I can't. "Oh, Eldora," I whisper. I fill the basin with water and bury my face in it. Finally, I wipe the water away and go back into the classroom. There is nothing else to do.

The class is quiet when I return, the only sound that of pens scratching back and forth across coarse paper. Mrs. Praeter gives me a sympathetic look.

The day is endless. I feel I should be someplace else, doing something else. But there is nothing to do and no place to go. I can't go to Eldora's. I just have to wait.

At lunchtime Florence invites me to her house to eat. I shake my head, the idea of lunch making me sick. But Florence isn't finished. She has something else to say.

"Leery," she offers. "They's better now, the class, than tafore." She hangs her head, letting her mousy hair hide her face. "You ken what I'm saying?" she asks.

I nod. I know what she's saying. Has Eldora made the difference? Or are we just growing up?

11

THE FINAL WEEKS of school, I stumble through class. School isn't fun without Eldora. Mrs. Praeter shakes her head and scolds me for not paying attention.

Finally the last day arrives. I drag myself up the steps and pull open the heavy front door, glad that the only thing left of school this year is Edward's graduation. That's tomorrow night. Edward is making the class speech and he practices all the time. For the last month all we hear at home is how students must make their own way in the world, how whether they succeed or fail is up to them. I don't know who else it would be up to but I don't say so.

The teachers let us out at noon today. Mostly all we do is clean desks, pick up leftover papers and write notes to one another. Nobody seems to mind.

I walk down the hallway to my classroom. Half way there, I stop and stare. What seems to be a cluster of butterflies is bobbing around by the coat rack. Eldora! I start to run, then I slow down, feeling shy. Maybe Eldora won't be the same.

"Mama quit drinking," Eldora tells me flat out the minute I get to her, like we had just been talking about her mother five minutes ago.

"The doctor says she's been really sad for a long time. He says with the medicine he gave her, she should be lots better and may not drink anymore."

I start to say something but Eldora's not finished. "Papa's talking about getting rid of the Red Deer."

That's probably a good thing, I'm thinking.

"Heidi's father talked to him but didn't say he wanted it." She laughs. "Wouldn't that be funny if he bought it?"

"He probably couldn't buy it even if he wanted to," I remind her. "Nobody has any money, probably not even Heidi's father." Eldora doesn't seem to know about money.

"But it would be funny," she says again and laughs.

I nod my head, agreeing with her. "It would be even funnier if he traded the feed store for it, though." I imagine what Heidi's face would look like if that happened.

Eldora giggles until her glasses slip almost off the end of her nose. "That's the best idea of all!" We laugh together until the final bell sends us into our seats.

Tending to wrapping up the school year takes the next hour or so: collecting papers and art projects and cleaning desks and blackboards. During this time, discipline is loose. We talk back and forth as we work.

"Quiet, class," says Mrs. Praeter, finally interrupting our chatter. "Please be seated."

"Next year you move upstairs, to the seventh-grade classroom," she begins. "You have completed the elementary level of your education. This means you are no longer children but young girls and boys. You will be expected to behave in a much more grown-up way." She stumbles over her words and pulls out a hanky. "Make me proud of you," she finishes.

I gulp, surprised to find that Mrs. Praeter will miss us. And even more surprised to find that I will miss her.

After her short speech Mrs. Praeter dismisses us and we take our leave. Eldora and I make plans to meet at the fort before she goes to visit her grandmother in Cincinnati. As I walk by Florence's house, I see her and yell: "See you next year." I vow next year I'll be friendlier.

"Hey, wait up, Leery." It's Sheldon. "What were you and Eldora whooping it up about?" he asks.

What we whooped about belongs to Eldora. "None of your business," I tell him and take off on a run for the creek.

"We'll see about that," he shouts, chasing after me. He catches up and in two bounds has picked me up and is swinging me out over the water. "Tell me or I'll drop you in."

"Sheldon, you're a nincompoop!" I yell. "Put me down."

He grins and stands me on the water's edge. "It's no matter to me anyway. I just figured it was a good way to rile you. I like to rile you, Leery."

"Sheldon, you're hopeless." I'm not mad, though. Funny how I'm not mad at him anymore.

He turns to go and I feel disappointed.

"I'd walk further with you, Leery," he says, like he read my mind. "But I have to get home. A mess of work around the farm in spring." With a wave he's off.

After Sheldon leaves I sit by the creek and take off my shoes and stockings. The grass tickles my toes as I walk. I stop for a minute to watch a yellow spider spinning a silvery web. A small breeze makes the web seem to dance. I think of the long summer ahead and happiness seems to bubble right up out of me.

*Folks who ain't got a pot to pee in hadn't
oughta be buyin' no new bicycles.*

12

EDWARD'S GRADUATION is over.
Everybody clapped a lot when he gave his
speech. Either they liked it a lot or they were
glad to be going home. That's where we're
headed.

"Stop spinning around! You're making me
dizzy!"

The spinning is me twirling around to
make my dress fly out. It flies out because
it's different from my other dresses. Those
couldn't fly if they had wings because they
fit like flour sacks which they probably are
because they came from welfare. The dress
I'm wearing came in a box of used clothes.

"Laura Grey!

It's Elizabeth who's complaining. I ignore her to show she can't boss me around all the time.

It's a warm June night, perfect weather. Edward's graduation didn't take a long time because there were only eleven students left in the class, mostly girls. A lot of the boys quit long ago to go to work. Mother wouldn't let Edward quit. Now that Thomas is sixteen he thinks he should be able to quit as well as do whatever else he wants. Mother won't let him do that either.

Tonight we're strung out like beads along the road. Up front are Thomas and my father. Father's home from being on the road. He came home for Edward's graduation. Father and Mother had a row last night about Father taking Thomas on the road to pick fruit this summer. Mother said she didn't want Thomas to be a bum and Father said are you calling me a bum and then they said a lot more. Father won, though, because everybody knows we need the money. Mother said they better be back by Labor Day.

Mother and Edward are next in line. Edward is trying to talk Mother into letting him buy Mr. Lambert's used car. Mr. Lambert, who owns the lumber yard where Edward got a job in the office, says Edward can pay a little each week. We don't have a car in our family. Edward has to talk Mother into going along with the idea because half of what everybody earns goes into the kitchen tin. If Edward buys the car, his half will probably go into the car instead of the tin.

Elizabeth and I bring up the rear, me twirling around and Elizabeth checking out the sky.

"Look," Elizabeth says. "There's the first star."

Seeing the first star means you can make a wish.

"What would you wish if you had seen it first?" Elizabeth asks.

"A bicycle," I answer, surprising myself. I never knew I wanted a bicycle. I've been saving for something, but I never knew it was a bicycle. They cost a lot of money.

"Sometimes I wonder if wishing on a star means anything," Elizabeth says. "You think God's up there?"

I look skyward. God has to be some place, I guess. Better up there than in the swamp with Gimpy McGee or in Alaska freezing to death.

"Sometimes I wonder." Elizabeth sighs. "I wished for a job for Father and a house for us."

I tell her instead of wishing for everything at once maybe she should start with something small, like an indoor toilet.

Elizabeth bursts out laughing. 'What a funny thing to say."

Elizabeth is serious, like Edward. That's probably why Mrs. Price who lives in Bloomfield where they still have money takes her to the lake all summer to watch over the twins. This will be Elizabeth's fourth year.

With Elizabeth and Thomas gone for the whole summer, it's going to be an empty house. Me? I have to go with Mother for two weeks in August when she fills in as a housekeeper. I want to stay home but she won't let me. She says I'm not old enough. How can I be old enough to watch over Violet but not old enough to watch over me?

"Come on, Elizabeth," I yell, starting to run. "The mosquitoes are after me." God never should have made mosquitoes.

When we get home, Thomas and Edward head out someplace or other and everybody else goes to bed.

Father and Thomas are gone when I get up in the morning. Father wanted to get on the road ahead of other hitchhikers. Elizabeth is sorting clothes to take to the lake. Edward's at the lumber yard and Mother's cleaning somebody's house.

Me? I'm going to work planting onions and tomatoes. I saw a sign at school last night that said Slovack's Farm needs planters. I can add to the three dollars and thirty-seven cents I've saved.

After breakfast I stop at Mrs. Willie's to see if Violet needs watching.

"Come tomorrow now," Mrs. Willie says, reminding me that tomorrow is her card club day. That's when I keep Violet outside so she doesn't get into trouble inside. I let Mrs. Willie know I haven't forgotten.

On my way to Slovack's Farm I cut through the field by Old Mrs. Lockgaar's house.

"Hey, come here, you dumb chickens!"

It's Benjoe, flapping his shirt and chasing after chickens. Benjoe and Thomas became best friends after Benjoe showed up in the subdivision one day from he never said where.

Mr. Zancowski lets him sleep in the back of his storeroom and help out around the store.

Benjoe spends a lot of time at our house. He runs out the back door when our mother comes in the front. That's because she feels strongly about people in the house when she's not home.

I ask Benjoe what he's up to.

"Thomas told me to ride herd on these chickens while he's gone." Benjoe laughs. His coal black hair tumbles over his forehead and his dark eyes sparkle with good humor. He always finds something to laugh about. In that way he and Thomas are a lot alike.

"Where you headed so early?" he asks.

"Planting," I tell him. "I'm saving money." I don't tell him why, still not believing why myself.

Just then a chicken flies over Old Mrs. Lockgaar's coop.

"See you," yells Benjoe, running after it.

Farmer Slovak's planting shed is filled with sacks of onions and flats of small tomato plants. Farmer Slovack, a man in faded overalls, his eyes shaded by a rumpled hat, sits outside the shed.

"These air the crops," he explains. "I pays thirty-five cents a row fer ernyons 'n fifty cents a row fer tomaters. You done this afor?" he asks me.

I shake my head.

"Then you'd best stick with ernyons." He gathers up a sack and pulls out a tiny onion: "See them whiskers?" He points to the root stubs on the bottom. Those air the feet. Feet goes down. Got that?"

I nod as I add in my head. I can earn a dollar and forty cents with four rows.

"The plowed rows air back there." He points to a fenced field. It's a long way. "Plant the feet good un tight and heads loose." He hands me a sack.

Dragging my sack behind me, I follow a well-worn path to the plowed field. There I shove my skirt above my knees and settle down to plant. The sun is warm on my back and the dirt soft and crumbly in my hands. I shove onions in, feet-first.

I work my way up the row, inching along the ground like a flowered worm. At the end I stand and stretch. Doing a row wasn't that bad. I can finish more than four.

At mid-day, I get a drink of water from the pump and notice the other planters are barefoot. I take off my shoes and socks and wiggle my toes in the dirt.

By early afternoon, I've done four rows. I want to do a fifth but the farmer won't let me. It's getting on to four o'clock, he says; time to quit. He gives me a dollar and forty cents, which I tie up in my handkerchief. I scrub my hands and face under the icy flow of the pump then head back to my rows to collect my shoes and socks.

"Hey there, Leery," calls a familiar voice. "I didn't know you planted."

Sitting on the back fence and looking like a red-haired scarecrow with a hammer stuck in his belt and a sack of nails over his shoulder is Sheldon.

"Our fields back up to Slovack's," he tells me. "I been fixing fences," he adds. "Are you headed home now, Leery?"

"Why do you call me Leery?" I suddenly want to know. "It's not my name. What's the matter with Laura?"

"It's big—and prissy—and you may be prissy but you sure aren't big." He laughs, teasing me, as always.

It's too nice a day to argue. "Yes, I'm headed home," I tell him. I tie my shoes together and swing them over my shoulder.

"You can cut through the back fields and catch up to the creek near school. I'll show you."

I try to decide. I would rather walk the fields than follow the road. The creek is back there some place. But Sheldon is a boy and boys are often up to no good.

"Leery, don't look like that. You think I'm gonna sic the bull on you?" He jumps off the fence and drapes my tied shoes around my neck pulling me close to him. "Come on," he says with a tug and a smile.

I duck under the shoes and run. In two seconds, I've climbed the fence and jumped down the other side. I race to the next fence line. Sheldon's right at my heels swinging my shoes in the air. I get to the fence first.

"Put your shoes on now, Leery," Sheldon advises, handing them to me. "There's prickers in the next field, strawberries, too, if you know where to look." He points back to where the fences cross one another.

I put my shoes and socks on, knowing there's nothing worse than a pricker in the foot. After I finish we crawl under the broken fence rails and head for the corner. Sheldon kneels down and separates the green tops of dozens of plants. The strawberries gleam bright red. They taste sun warm and tart sweet in my mouth.

Soon the shadows lengthen and it's time to go. Sheldon pulls me to my feet. His fingers are warm. We don't speak until we reach the creek near the school.

"Leery," Sheldon says, breaking the silence. "I'd walk further with you but it's supper time and Ma don't allow no late comers for supper." He lingers a while longer, then turns to leave.

"I've got to hurry along too," I tell him quickly. Then I feel bad, like I've cheated somehow. "Sheldon," I call after him. "The berries were really good."

He grins. "I'm glad you liked them, Leery. Like I said, I never intended to sic the bull on you." He starts to run off. Then he turns back: "Leery," he calls. "Do you ever go to the free show out back of the school in summer?"

"Sometimes," I answer. We went last year but the mosquitoes almost ate us alive.

"My pa sometimes takes a truckload of us over. I sure would like to see you there next time." He pauses, like he's waiting for an answer.

"Maybe," is all I can think to say.

"Yep," he yells. "You sure are prissy." He rumbles away like a giant bear, roaring and laughing all the way.

Sheldon is crazy but the strawberries were really good.

The rest of the way home I'm followed by squawking blackbirds returning to roost after a day spent stealing seeds. Eldora would have liked picking strawberries, I think. But not planting ernyons. I laugh. Then I stop, remembering Sheldon's saying I was prissy. I don't think I'm prissy.

The next day I get to Mrs. Willie's early. Violet and I settle in the pile of sand that was dumped behind her house a few years ago for nobody knows what. I make sand castles and Violet breaks them down. She laughs and I laugh along with her. I let the warm sand slide through my fingers, liking the way it feels.

"Hey, got room in that sand pile for one more?"

"Stop sneaking up on me like that," I snap at Benjoe, who just crept up from around the corner of the house.

He laughs. "I just delivered some things to Mrs. Willie. You looked like you were having fun. "Any word from Thomas?" He changes the subject so fast I don't have time to think up a smart answer.

"They're headed south to pick peaches," I tell him.

"He said he'd write me a letter so I can join the Navy,"

"That's silly. You can't join the Navy. You're too young." Nobody knows exactly how old Benjoe is because he never said but he looks about like Thomas.

"Just you wait." He does a sailor's jig that flips his dark hair back and forth across his forehead. "The Navy doesn't care how old you are. They just want a letter saying it's okay."

"You'd be better off in school," I tell him, sounding just like my mother.

"Got to go." He whistles his way through the fields.

I absentmindedly continue to make sand castles as I imagine Benjoe in a sailor suit twirling his white cap in his hand like a movie star.

13

THE SUMMER PASSES quicker than I like. Soon it's August and the tomatoes in the side yard turn red and the pears on the small tree in front turn yellow. Edward, now with his car, comes home from work, scrubs up behind the curtain in the kitchen and leaves. Mother and I think he has a girl.

One night Mother suggests we try the free show at school. "Maybe the mosquitoes won't be as bad this year," she says hopefully as she rubs citronella oil in her hair.

We walk to school and find a spot on the grass. A few cars and trucks are lined up behind us. Tinny music and black and white patterns on the screen announce the show is ready to start.

Just then an open truck with a sputtering engine charges between the screen and the projector. Everybody yells and whistles and honks until the truck moves.

"Hey Leery!" Everybody hushes and shushes.

It's Sheldon! I sink down on the ground, not wanting anybody to know it's me he's yelling at. That doesn't stop him. He jumps out of his truck, ducks under the projector light and comes up to me.

"Hi, Leery," he says in a happy voice.

"Be quiet," I whisper.

He drops down and I have to introduce him to my mother, for goodness sake, and she says hello and he says hello and everybody hushes us again.

"Come sit in the truck." Sheldon grabs my hand. "You can see better. Mrs. Grey, you can sit up front with Pa. Ma can't stand the picture show, says the jumpin' around makes her dizzy." He adds: "The mosquitoes aren't so bad when you're off the ground."

That does it for Mother. In two minutes she's up front in the truck and Sheldon's hoisted me into the back like I'm a sack of grain or something. Some of Sheldon's friends and a couple of younger brothers and sisters, intent on Rin Tin Tin, ignore us. Sheldon pulls me down close to him. I can feel the sunburn on his arm.

After the show, Sheldon lifts me down. I think he may tease me about a kiss, but he doesn't. I feel funny about that. Not that I want him to, but funny anyway.

Sheldon's father offers us a ride home. Mother says thanks but we like to walk. I'm glad. It's not that I'm ashamed of our house or anything; it's just easier not to have to explain the way we live. Besides, it's nobody's business.

"Another free show in two weeks," Sheldon says, a question in his voice.

"I'll be gone," I tell him, not saying where because that's nobody's business either.

"Well, Leery, then I guess I'll see you in school. You're not going away for that, are you?" He laughs.

"Don't be silly," I snap. Then I want to say something good about the free show but can't think of anything that wouldn't make me feel funny again. "The mosquitoes were lots better," I finally tell him.

Sheldon looks surprised then grins. "I'll keep them away from you any time, Leery," he says, leaning close and whispering right in my ear. His breath tickles and makes me shiver. I rub my ear and Sheldon laughs.

"I have to go," I tell him, hurrying to catch up to my mother who is trying to walk away from the mosquitoes.

Not too long after the free show a letter arrives from Eldora. She's coming home the end of August and wants me to meet her at our fort. There's also a letter from Thomas, not for us but for us to deliver to Benjoe. I run it over then wait while he opens it. He looks up and laughs. "You can go, Laura. I'm not joining the Navy until next year."

Feeling foolish, I race to Violet's house, where I'm supposed to take her for a walk. I don't know why I listen to anything Benjoe says. He talks crazy. Like the time he said God was coming when it was just the Northern Lights.

Mrs. Willie opens the door and hands Violet out. Her shoelaces aren't tied. I tie them for her. Violet's shoes are almost never tied. Mrs. Willie can't bend down and Violet won't lift her foot up.

Violet and I head down the dirt road that runs through the subdivision. We pass Ellen Allen's house. She's sitting outside on the ground. Ellen and I don't play as much as we used to. Neither one of us plays dress-up or paper dolls any more. We still see one another sometimes, though.

"I'm taking Violet for a walk. Want to come along?" I call out.

"Can't. I have to stay around the house." She turns away.

"If your father's not home, we can stay a minute," I say, pulling Violet along with me.

"No," Ellen says in a funny voice, turning her head back to us.

"Ohhh," says Violet, reaching out a hand to touch Ellen's cheek. It's shades of black and blue and a little yellow.

"Ellen!" I exclaim. "What happened?"

"Nothing." She pauses. "I fell."

"Oh?"

"It's nothing; I just fell," Ellen says again.

I don't know what to say so I say nothing but nothing must have been the right thing to say because Ellen whispers some more.

"Don't tell," she began.

Tell? What?

"Pa was gettin' after Ma and I got in the way of Pa's hand and Ma's head." She stops: "You won't tell, will you?"

"No, I won't tell," I assure her. But who's to tell? Everybody in the subdivision knows Ellen's father beats up on Ellen's mother.

Violet tries to touch Ellen's face again. Ellen jerks back, saying she has to go in. Before she leaves she comes close and whispers in my ear. "Pa says Violet should be sent away someplace."

I shake my head. Ellen's father should be sent away some place is what I'm thinking, but I don't say it.

Violet tugs on my hand and we continue our walk. When I return Violet home, Mrs. Willie gives me two dimes! That's a lot. I usually get the loose pennies that fall out of Mr. Willie's pockets when he sleeps on the couch after dinner, never more than five or six.

At home, I put one dime in the kitchen tin and the other in my cigar box.

14

TOO SOON IT'S TIME for Mother's housekeeping job at the Cresswells. They live in Bloomfield where Mother gets other jobs cleaning houses. She and I pack a few things and Edward drops us off. The Cresswell's house is big, like a mansion, although I've never seen a mansion.

Mrs. Cresswell seems nice. She shows us a big kitchen and then our room, Bridget's quarters, she calls it, which is just off the kitchen. It looks half the size of our house. There's a bed, a chest of drawers—big enough to hold all the clothes in our family—two lamps and a chair. Right next door is a bathroom just for us.

In the kitchen Mrs. Cresswell points to a bunch of buttons. They connect to all the rooms in the house so if somebody wants something they don't have to get up and walk through the whole house to get it. They push a button and my mother walks through the whole house to see what they want and then walks back through the whole house to get it for them.

As we talk, a boy and a girl come into the kitchen. They carry tennis rackets. The girl is bigger than I am, and heavier, with brown hair and dark eyes. She wears white pleated shorts. The boy is about my size, with brown hair cut very short. He is also dressed in white. Neither wears a welcoming look.

"This is our daughter Bethany and our son John. Bethany is just about your age, Laura. She was thirteen in May. John is twelve."

John frowns at this information, like it was private.

"Do you play tennis, Laura?" Mrs. Cresswell asks. "Bethany and John have been taking lessons this summer. If you didn't bring a racket, I'm sure we can find one for you."

I shake my head. Tennis? They only play tennis in movies, for goodness sake.

"Martha, I'll let you and Laura get settled," Mrs. Cresswell says. Martha is my mother's name although I never call her that. Mrs. Cresswell continues: "And Martha, you will want to know that Mr. Cresswell and I have dinner at eight o'clock. Bethany and John eat at five-thirty in the kitchen. You and Laura can eat with them. I know they will enjoy the company."

She goes out and John follows. Bethany holds back long enough to stick out her tongue, careful not to let my mother see.

Enjoy isn't the word I would use for two weeks with the Cresswells.

The first morning, right after breakfast, Bethany and John invite me to play hide-n-seek.

"You can be it," John says. "Count to a hundred."

Seems like a lot to me, but I hide my face in a pillar on the back porch and count off. It takes a long time to count to one hundred.

After I finish, I look for Bethany and John. There are lots of places to hide—the garage, the woodshed, behind bushes and up in trees. I even wander onto the tennis court.

Finally I yell "Allee-allee-incomefree!" That's what you're supposed to yell when you give up. "Allee-allee-incomefree!" I yell again. No answer. I sit on the back steps and wonder what to do.

"Lemonade?" Mother asks, carrying a glass. "You're probably looking for something to do now that Bethany and John have gone to the birthday party. I told Mrs. Cresswell how much you like to read and she said you can help yourself to the books in the library."

Birthday party! They never hid at all! What a dummy I am!

The library is paneled in dark wood and filled with books. I select Little Women and take it to my room where I manage to bury myself most of the week until Mother tells me I have to go outside.

With Bethany and John?

They want to play hide-n-seek again. I won't be fooled this time, only agreeing to play when John says he'll be 'it.' He counts and Bethany and I hide. She darts into the garage and I scurry behind a bush. I wait and wait. And wait.

Where are my brains? Of course nobody looks. Disgusted with myself, I walk back to the house. As I pass the garage, I notice the door open a crack. Remembering that Bethany hid there, I stick my head inside. A faint red glow comes from the corner. I recognize the smell of cigarettes because Thomas and Benjoe hide out and smoke them, too.

"Shut the door, dummy, so nobody sees us!"

John and Bethany are scrunched together, happily blowing smoke out their noses.

"You're smoking."

"Hey, maybe she's not so dumb after all," says Bethany.

"Keep quiet and we'll give you one," whispers John. "But pipe down."

"That's okay," I tell them. "I got to go."

"See, John," says Bethany, her voice following me as I scoot out the door. "She's chicken."

I walk into the kitchen and Mother hands me a chest of silver and some rags and silver cream. "How about polishing these for me?"

I sit at the kitchen table covered with newspapers and go to work. It's not a bad job but it turns your hands black. Mrs. Cresswell comes in and seems happy with how the silver looks.

The rest of the day is quiet. Only one more week, I'm thinking, one more week.

The next morning while I clean up the kitchen, Mother pulls our bed apart. Laundry day.

"Laura," Mother calls in a voice that doesn't sound good.

I hurry to the bedroom.

"Look what I found under your pillow," she says, holding up two cigarettes.

For goodness sake!

"You know anything about these?"

"I don't," I assure her.

"Throw them in the trash." She hands me the cigarettes, then laughs. "You wouldn't be so dumb as to hide cigarettes under your pillow." She goes back to stripping beds.

At dinner Bethany and John wear expectant looks on their faces. They glance at Mother and then at me.

"I'm glad nobody in this house smokes," Mother says suddenly. "Smoking makes you smell bad and turns your teeth black." She takes a small bite of meatloaf. "Don't you agree, Bethany, that it's nice nobody in this house smokes?"

Bethany gulps. "Yes," she mumbles.

John starts to giggle.

"Did you know, John?" Mother continues. "Smoking makes men lose their hair, usually at a very young age. Why sometimes, I believe, as young as you are."

John quits giggling. He looks at Mother and frowns but says nothing.

The next Saturday, the day before we are supposed to leave, Mr. Cresswell says Bethany and John and I can go to a matinee movie. The show starts at one o'clock. By noon I'm ready to go.

Mr. Cresswell drives us to town and gives each of us enough money for the movie and to buy popcorn at the dime store before we go in.

After we get our popcorn, Bethany and John run off. I look around, finally spotting Bethany at the lipstick counter.

"Laura, come here," Bethany calls. I go over to her, passing John in the candy aisle.

"What shade do you like?" Bethany asks. "I like this orange." She quickly drops a lipstick in her purse. "Take one. It's easy."

I can't do anything but shake my head. She's stealing!

"Don't be such a chicken." Bethany grabs my arm. "Everybody takes stuff."

I shake loose and run from the store. I try to hide in the movie but they find me and sit on either side. I feel squeezed.

Relieved to get home, I pick up my book and settle on the back steps to read. Behind me I hear the tinkle of ice cubes in a glass.

"You know you're a bookworm, don't you?" Bethany says.

A bookworm? Bookworms eat books. "I'm not eating your book," I tell her. Then I giggle. Maybe I am a bookworm. I devour books.

"Are you laughing at me?" Bethany demands.

"Are you laughing at my sister?" John joins in.

Before I can say a word, they pour ice water over my head and down my back, flooding the book I'm reading.

"I must have tripped," John says. "Sorry," not sounding a bit sorry.

"Oh, dear," Bethany says. "I'm so clumsy. I tripped, too."

I jump up and water flies off of me in all directions. I shake the now soaked book. I sputter, I stutter, I choke. Before I can stop myself, I yell: "You are brats! Worse than brats! You even steal from the dime store! And now you've ruined your own book!"

I've done it! Why can't I keep my mouth shut? I feel tears sting my eyes.

"I heard that!"

It's Mr. Cresswell. He's coming from the garage. He must have heard everything I said. There will be no more jobs like this for Mother.

"I'm sorry," I begin. Then I can't think of anything else to say. I can't say I didn't say what I just said when he already heard me say it.

"You two, come with me. We're going back to the dime store. I told you there was going to be no more of that, didn't I?"

"But it was Laura who stole things," yells Bethany.

"Yeah, it was Laura, not us," chimes in John "Just look in her pocket." He points at me.

My pocket? What's this? I shove my hand in the pocket of my dress. I pull out a tube of orange lipstick. I'm too shocked to speak.

116

"You can give that to me," says Mr. Cresswell, holding out his hand. "We've been through this before. Now, you two," he points to Bethany and John. "March right out to the car. And, John, you can hand over the candy bars. Or did you eat them already?"

John just looks down at his shoes.

"I thought as much."

The next thing I know they're gone.

I go inside to find Mrs. Cresswell and Mother in the kitchen. They heard everything.

"Martha, I'll take you and Laura to the bus tonight," Mrs. Cresswell is saying. "There's no need for you to wait until tomorrow. I am sure we can manage until Bridget gets back on Monday."

Mother and I pack. Now there will be no bonus for Mother and probably no pay for Sunday.

As we're leaving, Mrs. Cresswell hands Mother an envelope: "Here is your two weeks pay, Martha, and the bonus I promised you. I've included a dollar for Laura for the nice job she did on the silverware."

A dollar! I smile, happy for the first time since moving in with the Cresswells.

"I guess indoor toilets aren't everything," I tell Mother once we get home.

The end of August comes. It's Monday and Eldora is waiting at the fort. I rush around cleaning and filling lamps—my inside job— and scrubbing down the outhouse toilet seats—my outside job. On my way to Eldora's I cut through fields of bright blue chicory and white Queen Anne's lace. I pick a bouquet.

I reach the fort and Eldora yelps happily as I drop through the roof. The fort is already alight with candles in tin cans. Books fill orange crates. A new rug is on the floor, a real rug instead of Eldora's old coat. Eldora has been cleaning. Dust hides the freckles on her face and cob webs put gray streaks in her dark hair.

"Where is your hair bow!" I yell when I realize that the only thing on Eldora's head is a dusty web.

"I told Papa I'm getting too old for silly hair bows."

"Here," I hand her the flowers. "You can put these in your hair instead."

We both laugh and pile the flowers in a tin can.

Eldora says her summer was filled with concerts and plays and museums and opera. Her grandmother made her go so often that the only way she could stay home was to pretend to be sick.

I stayed home a lot, I tell her. Except for two weeks of housekeeping with my mother.

Eldora giggles as I tell her about Bethany and John and the cigarettes under my pillow and the stolen lipstick in my pocket. "Oh, how I wish I had been there," she says. "We could have fixed them good."

Before Eldora can tell me how she would have fixed Bethany and John, a boat horn that's loud enough to wake the dead, calls her to dinner.

We say our good-bys and climb back through the roof.

I head home, thinking of my birthday the next day. Thirteen seems a lot older than twelve.

15

I WAKE UP not feeling older. That's probably because I turned thirteen at two o'clock in the morning and wasn't awake to notice the difference.

Downstairs a note from Mother wishes me a happy birthday and tells me that cinnamon toast is in the kitchen oven. She'll be home early, she says.

After breakfast I check my cigar box. I count every penny but it still adds up to only five dollars and seventeen cents. Not enough for a bicycle. I don't feel bad about it, though, because I never knew I wanted one.

After I do my chores, I take a book outside under the pear tree. A warm September sun colors everything gold and I wish I could bottle it up for winter.

I must have fallen asleep because a shadow falling across my face wakes me up.

"Hi, Laura."

It's Ellen and I'm glad to see her.

"Today's your birthday," Ellen says, which is no surprise to me but a surprise that she knows it.

"Don't you remember? Your ma bought a pint of strawberry ice cream last birthday and we ate it in your back yard." She sighs. "That was afore your ma and my pa got into it with one another."

I'm surprised to find out how pleased I am that Ellen remembers.

"That was fun," she adds. "Oh, I brought you a present." She reaches in her pocket and pulls out a silver tube of lipstick.

I back away, like it's something that will bite me.

"It's lipstick," she says, handing it to me. "Cherry. The lady in the dime store said it was the most popular color."

"I'm glad it's not orange," I say, without thinking. Then I have to make up a reason why I'm glad it's not orange and that's not easy to do. The best I can think of is that orange looks too orange. Ellen doesn't seem to think this is strange. I do.

Ellen droops a little and sighs. "I bought it for me. Ma said it was all right but Pa said it made me look like a streetwalker and I couldn't keep it."

I open the tube. It's cherry all right, bright red and shiny. I stare at it.

"Ain't you going to try it?" Ellen asks. She takes the lipstick. "I'll put it on for you. I practiced some before Pa made me give it away."

"I want to do it myself," I say, not meaning it. Nobody I know wears lipstick, not even my mother.

"Well, I have to go," Ellen says, handing me the lipstick. "I have to get home to help Ma with supper. It has to be on the table when Pa gets home or he gets mad."

"It's nice, Ellen," I tell her. "Really. And I like it a lot."

She smiles. "I'm glad you like it. Maybe we can try it out together some time." She waves and is gone.

I drop the lipstick in my pocket and sit back down in the grass. I pick up my book but can't concentrate. After awhile my hand finds its way to my pocket. I finger the lipstick. Nobody wears lipstick—just girls in peek-a-boo blouses.

I hurry inside and run up the attic steps. A small mirror hangs on the wall. I study my face. The nose is pointy but the lips look normal.

I take the cap off the lipstick and roll up the tube. A sweet, greasy smell fills the warm room. How to go about this? I draw a line from the bow of my lips on the right side to the corner of my mouth. I do the same on the left side. I fill in both sides. It's not hard to do, like coloring maps in school. You just have to stay within the lines. I paint the bottom lip. Then I smack my lips the way they do in the movies.

I look older, lots older. I pucker my lips.

"Oh, not now, Charles," I protest. "You'll smear my lipstick."

I giggle, glad there's nobody around to hear me. I admire my face. It looks so much older. Maybe it's not just the lipstick. Maybe it's being thirteen. As I'm thinking about this, I notice the right side of my mouth is a tiny bit higher than the left. I balance things up by adding a dab of lipstick to the left side. Now the right side looks higher. I dab a little on the left. Maybe this isn't as easy as

125

coloring maps. The more I try to fix things, the worse it gets.

I decide my mouth belongs on a clown. I draw red circles on my cheeks and triangles over my eyes. I add a cherry lipstick nose. The clown smiles. I like the way it looks and am working on other clown expressions when I hear the front door open.

"Laura! Are you home?"

It's Elizabeth! She wasn't supposed to be back before Labor Day. I race down the steps. "Elizabeth! What are you doing home?"

"I live here. And *what's* on your face?"

I cover my face with my hands, suddenly remembering what I look like. "Just practicing for Halloween," I explain, not thinking for a minute that she'll believe me.

She laughs: "Looks more like you've been playing cowboys and Indians. Better get that stuff off before Mother comes home."

I run to the kitchen and pump water into a basin. Using the soap Mother makes in the back yard—strong enough to take the skin off a mule, Thomas says—I scrub away.

"Better, but not by much," Elizabeth comments when I come back.

Just then a car pulls out front.

"Quick, cover your eyes!" Elizabeth cries. "Hurry!"

I do as I'm told. The front door opens and I hear whispers. Something smells funny, like oil.

Elizabeth pulls my hands away.

Everybody—Mother, Father, Thomas, Edward, Elizabeth—are all standing around looking at me. They're smiling.

I blink. In front of me is a new, blue as a summer sky, bicycle.

"Happy Birthday!"

Tears sting my eyes and I can't think of one thing to say. I know how much everybody must have sacrificed to buy such a gift for me.

"We all knew how much you wanted a bicycle," comments Father. "We've been saving up."

"Everybody came home early just to be here today, Laura," Mother says.

"Don't you want to try it out?" Thomas asks.

"Better get going before it gets dark," Elizabeth advises.

"I'll help you wheel it out," Edward offers. "I know you can ride. You learned on that old bicycle of mine before it fell apart."

I wheel the bicycle to the dirt road. Will I remember how to ride, I wonder. I sit on the seat and push down on the petals. I move slowly, wobbling back and forth across the road like a chicken with its head cut off. I keep at it and after awhile there's less wobble. Finally I'm steering a straight line in the road.

I pass Ellen's house as her father climbs from the ditch where he dumps the family trash. He stops dead in front of me and I stop dead behind him. I go flying in the ditch. Luckily my bicycle lands on top of me.

Mr. Allen frowns. He walks over and looks down at me.

"That a new bicycle?" he finally asks.

I nod, afraid to speak.

He stands there continuing to stare. Finally he shakes his head: "Folks who ain't got a pot to pee in hadn't oughta be buying no new bicycles."

He turns, spits a stream of tobacco juice across the road and heads back into the house.

My mouth drops open. I've never seen anybody spit so far.

I brush dirt off my bicycle and myself, neither of us any worse for wear. Then I continue my wobble down the road. By the time I get home, the wobble is gone.

"Just in time," Mother calls as I lean my bicycle against the wall outside the door.

Dinner's on the table and everybody's talking, as usual. Tonight I surprise myself and everybody else. "Folks who ain't got a pot to pee in hadn't oughta be buying no new bicycles." I repeat Mr. Allen word-for-word and try to sound as much like him as I can. The whole family stops eating and stares at me.

I wait. I look around the table. Suddenly everybody's grinning from ear to ear.

"Hadn't oughta be buying no new bicycles," Thomas yells, pounding on the table. Everybody starts laughing.

Mother mutters: "That man!" but laughs right along with the rest of us.

We sit around and talk until Mother says it's time for everybody to go to bed because she's tired.

We're just getting up from the table when there's a bam-bam on the door. Thomas opens it to a winded looking Ellen Allen.

"Pa's gettin' into Ma something awful," she exclaims. "He got into the drink," she adds, like that explains something.

"Hoodlum," Mother comments. "You stay here, Ellen. We'll see what's going on."

"Now, Martha, no need for you to get into this," says my father. "Edward and I can handle things."

"No need!" Mother exclaims. "That man needs to be taught a lesson. And I'm going to see that he gets one."

As there is no arguing with Mother when her mind is made up, she goes. Elizabeth and Ellen and I wonder and wait.

After a short time, too short for much of a lesson, everybody but Mother returns. Father says Mr. Allen was in bed sleeping it off when they got there, that if we wait a bit it'll be okay for Ellen to go home. He doesn't say what Mr. Allen was sleeping off. He says Mother stayed behind to talk with Mrs.

Allen. When Mother gets home she wears a satisfied look on her face.

The next day I hear that when Mr. Allen got up from sleeping it off he found he was missing his wife, his daughter, his truck and his wallet. I know about the wife, the daughter and the truck. I don't know about the wallet. I haven't seen Mr. Allen around either, though nobody said he was missing.

What do you think One Eye would do if he found his boys were stealing his beer?

16

NOW THAT SCHOOL'S STARTED I had to find someplace for my new bicycle. First I parked it in the kitchen. Mother made me take it out. Then I parked it inside the front door. She didn't like that either. Finally, Old Mrs. Lockgaar said I could leave it with her chickens in the shed. I know. Chickens aren't good company for bicycles but rain and snow are worse.

Anyway, school's started up again and that means winter's here. Well, not exactly here this minute but it may as well be because once school comes winter's right behind. There's nothing in the middle but

Halloween. Dressing up on Halloween and going around yelling help the poor until somebody comes to their door and gives you candy or something is the best thing before winter.

I haven't decided what I want to be this year. Last year I was a scarecrow but the straw in my sleeves and neck almost itched me to death. I want to be a ghost but can't find an old sheet that's not on somebody's bed.

I'll come up with something because I never miss going begging on Halloween. Sometimes I fill almost half a sack by yelling help the poor at every house in the county. Usually I get a piece of candy or an apple, sometimes a penny or two. One time I got a potato, which wasn't much fun, but I took it home anyway.

I want to keep thinking Halloween this morning but school keeps coming into my head no matter how many times I tell it to stay out. First, I'm in seventh grade this year and that means upstairs with all the big grades. That's where everybody eats in one big room at lunch time and there's no place left for seventh grade so they have to eat on the floor. That's what Thomas told me this morning.

Then I'm thinking about Elizabeth's blouse that I put on this morning for my first day of school, the one with the big puffy sleeves. What made me do it? The puffs are too puffy and my arms are too skinny. Last of all I'm thinking about Sheldon who made me feel funny when he whispered in my ear. Will I feel funny when I see him?

The sun feels warm and I linger on the school steps. Finally the first bell rings and I have to go inside. When I get upstairs I spot Eldora washing a rock in the drinking fountain. The front of her dress is covered with dirt. Eldora doesn't care what she wears but I've never seen dirt on her clothes before.

"Look what I found, Laura." Eldora opens her hand.

"A rock?" I ask, then add: "What happened to you?" pointing to the front of her dress.

"This is not just a rock, Laura. This is a fossil." Eldora's excitement wrinkles her nose like a rabbit's. "I found it in Florence's front yard in a big pile of rocks."

Rocks?

"Look." Eldora holds the rock out again. "It's a trilobite."

I look but can only see marks left by a chicken.

"Those are fossil marks," Eldora tells me, dropping the rock in my hand. "You are holding a rock that an ancient creature died on a million years ago."

I wish I thought it was as exciting as Eldora does. I hand the rock back and Eldora wipes it on the front of her dress and drops it in her pocket. Then we head for our new classroom halfway down the upstairs hall.

"What was the pile of rocks doing in Florence's front yard?" I ask, wondering how I missed seeing the pile and then wondering where I am when I miss things like that.

Eldora shrugs her shoulders, letting me know rocks in Florence's yard are only of interest in fossil hunting.

We reach the seventh grade classroom and go inside. It looks about the same as the sixth grade classroom except the desks can be moved around. Up front is what looks like a big window shade hanging over the blackboard but is really a map when you pull it down.

The last bell hasn't rung yet but it looks like almost everybody is there except Miss Olaf, our new teacher.

I aim for my usual place at the back of the room but Eldora grabs my arm. "You can't see anything from back there," she tells me, pointing to two empty desks up front. I like not being seen but I follow her.

The class looks different, the same students yet not the same. The boys look taller and Fat Eddie isn't fat any more. Heidi has let her hair grow and there's a big bow in back instead of on the side. Only Rosemary looks the same; beautiful and golden in her yellow sweater and yellow curls. Sheldon is nowhere to be seen.

A movement at the door and a gasp from somewhere in the room makes me look that way. It's Florence, but a Florence no one has ever seen before, one with a fluffy sweater and bright pink lipstick! As she walks to her favorite place by the window, the entire class follows her with their eyes.

"Is it Halloween?" a voice from the back of the room asks. "Must be," comes the reply, "because the witches are out."

Florence doesn't turn around, just gazes out the window.

I can't help but stare, taken by the strangeness of this new Florence. She's still skinny but her old sweater is gone, replaced by a furry pink one that covers what looks like a peek-a-boo blouse, a blouse with two ties at the neck and a slit below! Her lank hair is up and rolled over a wire and brush holder; a rat, I think it's called. And with the lipstick she looks lots older. She turns to see my eyes on her and flushes a little. I wave hello and she smiles and waves back.

Eldora ignores the commotion over Florence to return to the examination of her stone. I wonder again what the stones were doing in Florence's yard. There hadn't been anything new but babies in that yard in all the times I've walked by.

I quit wondering anything as the final bell rings and Miss Olaf marches into the classroom. She closes the door firmly behind her and moves front and center where she appears to examine the class for flaws, of which she must have seen a lot from the expression on her face.

"Welcome to seventh grade," she says. "My name is Miss Olaf."

Miss Olaf is a commanding figure in a wide shouldered and wide lapelled dark suit. On her lapel is pinned a seahorse made of green glass. It appears to ride the waves of her jacket as she moves. Her feet are big and sensibly settled in brown tie shoes, which is a good thing as she marches back and forth across the room a lot. Her hair could have been a model for Florence, rat, roll and all.

This is Miss Olaf's first year at Red Ridge School. She came back home to live with her brother after his wife died from a broken neck after falling out of the rafters in the barn.

"You seventh grade students are no longer children," Miss Olaf begins. "You are no longer playing at learning. You are young men and women ready to become adults. It is my job to see that you learn well." She stops. "You," she points at Eldora. "Is that rock more important than what I have to say?"

Eldora pales and has the good sense not to respond.

"Don't let me see anyone's eyes directed any place except toward me when I am talking to you," she says. "That is the first rule of this class: Everyone will play strict attention when anyone is speaking. Rule number two: Everyone will be seated ready for work then the final bell rings. Rule number three: All homework will be handed in on time. Finally," she adds: "We are going to learn to write this year, clearly, correctly and concisely—and we are going to learn to think the same way. In order to see if you are learning how to write, I will expect a weekly one-page report on the current book you are reading. If you are sick, send your work in anyway. If you are kicked in the head by a horse, I might understand." She pauses: "Then again, I might not."

I think I see a slight twitch around her left eye when she says about the horse.

The morning goes fast and when it's over, Eldora leaves for lunch and I stand at the door of the large study room upstairs watching students opening lunch bags, boxes and tins. Elizabeth is sitting in the middle of a bunch of seniors. I don't see Thomas any place.

A whiff of some combination of vanilla and laundry soap and a small voice tells me Florence is speaking to me. Other things may have changed about Florence but not her whispers.

"Would yer like ter brung yer lunch ter my place, Laura?" she asks. "We's a new table out ta back 'n we kin et thar. It's real purty." Her voice dies away. "My ma and new paw" she says this with some pride, "took the youngens to git skool rags as they be too busy afore."

I find myself heading to Florence's house where it looks the same, except for the pile of stones out front. Florence leads me out back.

"The here is our Californey yard," she says and points to a back yard completely covered by stones. "Better'n grass, Harold says. They's no mowin er nothin."

In the middle of the yard is a red picnic table graced by a bowl of fruitflies. Overhead, protecting the flies from the mid-day sun is a giant red and white stripped umbrella.

"Ain't it something, Leery?" whispers Florence. "Ma 'n Harold bought everything Satiday, jest after they be wed."

This is a surprise to me because I thought Florence's mother was already wed, what with the babies and all. "It's really something," I agree with Florence. "Really something."

"Harold works regular, Leery," Florence says proudly. 'He buys stuff for us, clothes 'n everything."

We work our way through lunch, Florence having cereal and me having a peanut butter sandwich. I drop my empty bag on top of the fruitfly bowl, hoping to block returns. The fringe on the big umbrella flaps in the breeze.

It's nice. Maybe it is like California; I've never been there.

Florence and I are just leaving when a car pulls up in front and a bunch of squealing voices come out of it. It's Florence's mother with children and new husband. He climbs from the car, about twice the size of his wife who is about the size of a china doll and as pretty. The babies fly around the yard and Florence's mother charges after them like a banty hen.

"Now, Matty, leave 'em be," says Harold pulling her into the fold of his arm. "Leave 'em be. They'll foller they mama."

Harold is right because he and Florence's mother go into the house and the rest follow.

As for Florence and me, we head back to school. "That's really something," I tell Florence again. Florence nods her head in agreement.

After school Eldora makes me look at her rock again, informing me that she intends to add it to her collection in our fort. Eldora's rock collection takes up one whole shelf of an orange crate. Some of the stones are interesting shapes and I once told Eldora they would be prettier if she painted them. When I saw the look on her face I didn't suggest it again.

17

IT DOESN'T TAKE LONG for the class to get used to Miss Olaf and her militant ways. We learn that she means it when she says we will work. We also learn that Miss Olaf likes to read plays aloud, which she does for fifteen minutes every Friday afternoon, taking all the parts with gusto.

I find myself trying to puzzle through what an adverb is and how you can tell if a participle dangles or not. Then there is the mysterious process called the diagramming of a sentence, a process in which entire sentences are torn apart to where they make no sense at all.

Having Opinions is important to Miss Olaf. She insists that everybody have one about the assigned readings. Opinions need not be long, but when called upon no one gets away with not having one. And nobody better laugh at an Opinion. Miss Olaf gets very upset and sends students to the blackboard to stand with their nose in a circle for such an infraction.

I never would laugh at an Opinion and I always have one of my own. How can you read something and not have an Opinion? Some of my Opinions make Miss Olaf's eyebrows go up or her mouth twitch but she just nods her head in appreciation.

As for Florence, the boys' reaction to her seems to have shifted from jokes to something else. I don't pay too much attention until one day in early October when Sheldon shows up in class.

Miss Olaf welcomes him, saying she understands the life of the farmer and that he should see her after class to catch up.

Sheldon flushes red, probably embarrassed by the attention. I notice he's wearing his father's sweater as he often does. Only this time it fits. I wonder if he's ever going to stop growing. His red hair is slicked back, like he stuck his head in the horse trough, and his freckles glow from a combination of sun and embarrassment.

My mind wanders a lot in the morning and my Opinion isn't as good as it should be on whether the man was brave or stupid, the one who builds a fire under a snowy tree in the Jack London story. Only Miss Olaf doesn't say stupid, she says unwise.

Miss Olaf doesn't call on Sheldon, and it's a good thing because he has discovered Florence and can't take his eyes off of her. Florence turns to see him watching. Then for some reason she has to retie her blouse, which turns Sheldon an even brighter shade of red. Miss Olaf notices and asks him if he doesn't feel well.

He is looking worse than ill and I am beginning to enjoy watching him. Suddenly something inside me begins to twitch. It starts around the middle of my stomach; it grows and fights its way up my rib cage; it wobbles up and down in my throat. I choke trying to hold it back. It escapes. First a tiny giggle comes out, then a snuffle, then a snort, and finally a noisy, outburst of laughter! Right in the middle of Heidi's Opinion!

Eldora looks at me in surprise.

So does Miss Olaf. "Laura, I am certainly surprised."

Not as surprised as I am.

Miss Olaf motions me to the board and the circle in chalk. I stand on rubbery legs.

"That laugh was discourteous and unkind," Miss Olaf scolds.

Nothing like this has ever happened to me before. I walk to the blackboard and the dreaded circle, seeing it only through blurred vision. Maybe the shame will kill me and I won't have to go through with it. Suddenly I know I can never do it, I can never place my nose in that circle. I turn and, while the entire class watches, walk out the door.

What am I doing, I ask myself? Where am I going? I stand outside the classroom feeling sick and scared. How can I put my nose in that hated circle? How could I have done something so awful that I had to do it? I wait for what seems like hours. Nobody comes, not Miss Olaf, not the principal, not even one of the students. Finally, I decide I have to go back. There is no place else for me to go. I open the classroom door and slide inside. I hope nobody sees me.

Miss Olaf is talking: "Story problems are more than faceless numbers. They are numbers of substance, numbers with meaning. Thirty

150

is no longer thirty; it is thirty miles or thirty ears of corn." She doesn't look my way. No one else dares look my way either. I glance at the clock, surprised to see I haven't been gone five minutes. I walk to the blackboard and stand in front of the hated circle. My hands are clenched in hot, sweaty balls. I lean my nose to the board and close my eyes. I stand there frozen for an eternity, until Miss Olaf lets me go: "You may take your seat, Laura."

I don't look at anyone, just stay scrunched in my seat until the lunch bell rings. As I stand to leave, Miss Olaf calls me to her desk.

"Leaving was unwise, but returning was brave," she says, with a slight twitch at the corner of her mouth.

As this is hardly what I expected, I offer an explanation. "I wasn't laughing at Heidi, Miss Olaf," I exclaim. "I wouldn't laugh at an Opinion; I was just...." I trailed off, not wanting to say more.

Miss Olaf's interest wasn't in the cause of the laughter, only the results. "You may know you were not laughing at Heidi, but she did not. We must be careful how our actions appear to others."

Thinking I'm dismissed, I begin to leave.

But Miss Olaf isn't finished: "I would like you to stay after school today to write an essay on why leaving the room was a poor choice. That is all; you may leave now."

Eldora is waiting for me outside the classroom.

"Heidi would never think I was laughing at her," I say as soon as the door closes behind me.

"You don't have to see the principal, do you?" Eldora asks anxiously.

As seeing the principal is the worst possible thing that could happen to anybody, I can see why she is worried. No one knows what happens when you see the principal, but it must be something awful.

"No, I just have to stay after school to write something for Miss Olaf," I answer, not wanting to share my shame any further.

"That's not bad," Eldora tells me as she heads off to lunch. I get my lunch and a book and head outside, planning to sit by the creek. In warm weather it's a good place to sit. As I settle down on the dry grass a slight breeze sends yellow leaves into the water where they twirl around like tiny boats. I wonder if I'll ever live down my shame.

After lunch I walk back to school and stand on the steps waiting for the bell to ring. To my surprise, Fat Eddie comes up to me and tells me I'm lucky I have such a small nose. Rosemary pats me on the shoulder and tells me how brave I am. Somehow, my misadventure of the morning isn't turning out the way I expected.

Sheldon, who is still having trouble keeping his eyes off Florence, finally takes the time to come over. He demands that I tell him what I was laughing at. "It couldn't have been Heidi's Opinion because it wasn't any dumber than any of her others."

I don't answer him. I'm angry, and sad and disappointed, all at once, and I don't know why. I turn away. Maybe I'm coming down with consumption. I'll have to quit school and go to Switzerland and sit in bed all day staring out the window and spitting blood into a handkerchief.

After school, I write my essay and hand it in to Miss Olaf. She reads it while I wait. Finally, she nods her approval and I am free to go. I want to tell her again how sorry I am, but she stops me. "We all make mistakes, Laura," she tells me, waving me off with a kind smile.

I leave, still feeling unsettled. When I reach the creek, I'm deciding whether I want to jump the rocks for probably the last time this year. Before he says a word I can feel him behind me.

"What are you mad at, Leery?" he demands. "What did I do?"

Am I mad? If I am mad I don't know it. I don't know what I am.

"It's nothing," I tell him. "And I'm not mad." Maybe I'm sad. Maybe it's fall. Fall is always sad because it means winter is coming.

"I'm glad you're not mad," Sheldon says. "Come on," he adds. "I'll walk you aways." He takes my hand and I pretend not to notice.

"I might not come to school anymore, Leery," he says suddenly. " I'm getting too old; fifteen next month. Besides, everything I need to know I can learn on the farm." He bends over my head and I can feel his breath ruffling the ends of my hair, gentle as a night breeze.

"There's good things, though, in school, Leery. Things I would miss." He ducks his head and looks right into my eyes.

I'm startled by how close his face is to mine, by the questioning look in his blue eyes.

"Would you miss me, Leery?" he asks softly.

My face feels hot. I don't know what to say. "You should go to school," I tell him, ignoring the question. "You told me yourself that there's not much to do on the farm in winter."

Suddenly he crushes a handful of leaves and drops them in my hair. "I'd come back just to tease you, Leery," he says with a laugh.

I shake leaves out of my hair.

"Gotta run, Leery," he says, giving my hand a squeeze like he wants to take it with him. He stays a little longer before running off.

18

SHELDON DOESN'T come back to school through the entire harvest season. As the last day of October arrives and I still don't see him, I begin to wonder if he meant it, about quitting.

But I have other things on my mind. It's Halloween and I still haven't come up with anything special to wear begging. I can always go as a bum but almost everybody goes as a bum and I wanted to be something different.

Eldora says begging is silly and, besides, she can eat all the candy she wants because her father puts it out and nobody ever comes.

But candy is not what Eldora is thinking of this morning as she beckons me to join her in the cloak room down the hall. She's muttering and sputtering like I have never seen her. Her freckles are jumping up and down on her nose like water on a hot stove.

"I'll get them," Eldora says. "I'll get them good!"

She will, too. Whatever needs getting, I know Eldora can do it.

"Get what, who?" I ask, as we hang up our damp coats and wait for the bell to ring. It's raining outside and the narrow locker room smells of wet wool and miserable weather. I shiver.

Eldora leans close and whispers: "Laura, somebody's been using our fort!" She shakes her head back and forth, so angry her glasses almost fall off.

Our fort! "How do you know?" I ask.

"Little things," Eldora says mysteriously. "Things that nobody would hardly notice—

candles slightly burned, the roof not on right, like that."

I start to say something but Eldora's not finished.

"Then cigarette butts, Laura! Cigarette butts crushed out on our carpet!"

Cigarette butts on our carpet is the worst thing, our carpet being a real rug now instead of Eldora's old winter coat.

"Who could it be?" I wonder.

We decide it's nobody in our class because if anybody had found our fort and was using it, everybody would know it, including us.

I think of the Klewicki boys but I can't see them climbing into our fort; they would just tear it down.

"We're going to find out who it is," Eldora says. "We're going to stand watch tonight and every night until they come."

Tonight!

"Tonight is Halloween and I'm going begging," I remind Eldora. "Besides, I don't like the woods at night and I'm not going to sit out there." I pause. "And neither should you. You'll get pneumonia." I stop, unable to think of anything else.

"Then how are we going to find out who's using our fort, who's burning up our candles and who's ruining our rug with their cigarette butts?" asks Eldora. "And how are we going to take care of them if we don't know who they are?"

It's a good question and I wish I had an answer. "I'm not going to sit in the woods on Halloween night," I tell her again.

"But Halloween night might be the best time to catch them," Eldora pleads. "Maybe we can scare them to death."

"I'm not scaring anybody. I'm going begging. And that's that." To my ears I sound emphatic.

I guess I'm not emphatic enough because less than twelve hours later I'm sitting on the cold ground behind some prickly bushes wrapped in an old horse blanket belonging to Eldora's father with stove soot smeared all over my face..

"This is crazy," I begin, for the tenth time.

"Shhhh," Eldora whispers. "I think I hear something."

I strain my ears but don't hear a thing but the rustle of some night animal and hope it's not a skunk.

We wait, neither of us saying a word, but nobody comes.

"It was nothing," I tell Eldora. "Nobody's coming. I can still go begging if I go now. I'll just go with this black face as my costume." This may work out all right, I'm thinking.

"Hush," she tells me. "I know...." she suddenly stops what she's saying.

Now I can hear it, too. Somebody is coming! Goosebumps crawl up and down my back. I don't like this. What am I doing here? As I shiver and wonder, three figures appear.

A giggle and a whisper of a voice: "They's a party out ta heer? A Halloween party in the woods?"

"Florence!" I almost forget to whisper.

"Shhhhh," Eldora cautions.

"Nah. Party's not here," says Clarence, the oldest Klewicki brother. "We's gonna have air own little party first. Pull off that roof, Darrell," he orders his brother.

Florence! With the Klewicki boys!

"You wanna see our fort, don'tcha?" says Darrell, working on the roof. "You wanna see what we got stashed inside? Ya like beer, dontcha? We got Stroh's swiped right offen Paw's front stoop," he brags.

"Beer!" Florence's whispery voice rises: "I ain't drinkin'no beer. Ma sez beer's jest pee water. They ain't no party ta here neither. They was niver a party." She sounds so sad I almost want to call out to her.

"Hey!" Darrell yells. "We is too havin' a party." A giggle. "No, we three is havin' a party?" He laughs at his own joke. "Dontcha like small parties?"

"You'ns kin have yer own party—they's no party ta here for me." Florence's voice gets even smaller and she runs off. Run, Florence, run, I want to yell.

"Florence is leaving," I whisper needlessly as we watch her go.

"Their fort!" Eldora whispers back, clearly hearing only what she considers the most important thing. .

"Aw let her go, Darrell," says Clarence. "They's more Strohs for us 'thout that skinny stick lappin it all up." He drops into the fort and his brother follows.

"We aren't going to scare them," I whisper.

"Can't scare the Klewicki boys," Eldora agrees.

Our fort! We huddle together in misery.

"We don't have to scare them," I begin, thinking out loud. "All we have to do is tell."

Eldora looks at me like she thinks the cold has frozen my brain. "Tell?"

"Course we would have to get a message out some how, tell without us doing the telling." I can't see how to do this, though.

"Go on," Eldora encourages, wiping coal dust off her glasses using a little spit for polish.

"What do you think One Eye would do if he found out his boys were stealing his beer?" I ask.

Eldora is quiet, then gives a soft laugh, like Dracula. "He'd kill 'em," she whispers. "He'd skin em alive." She stands up grabbing the blankets. "Let's go; we need pencil and paper."

We run to Eldora's where she sneaks in her back door and returns with pencil and paper and flashlight. We write and rewrite the note. Finally, by ten o'clock Eldora is satisfied.

*The beer stolen by Darrell and Clarence
is at Eldora's fort in the woods behind
her house. Better be quick because
they're drinking it up like crazy.*

19

ELDORA AND I TRY to be as quiet as field mice as we creep through the woods toward Klewicki's shack. We needn't have bothered. When we get close, we hear men's voices, loud and full of cuss words, a poker game by the sounds of it. We crouch down behind some bushes, not certain what we want to do now that we're here.

Eldora points to a woodpile near the front porch and begins to crawl that way. She turns back to look at me, the whites of her eyes in her coal-smeared face, commanding me to follow. We make our way across the dirt yard and behind the stack of wood where we can clearly see the front porch. Beer bottles are stacked up by the door alongside a pile of empty tin cans and what looks like a dead dog but is probably just a pile of burlap bags. Empty oil drums and their lids are scattered around the dirt of the yard.

My teeth chatter from the cold and my knees knock from fear, both so loud I'm afraid everybody inside can hear.

"Now what?" I whisper.

"Now what what," answers Eldora. She hands me the note. "Here."

"What am I supposed to do with it?"

"Get it read. What do you think? It was your good idea."

Get it read? How? I can't just walk up to the door and say here read this. "What if I wrap it around a rock and throw it at the door?"

Eldora looks at me like I've lost my mind.

"Well, it could work," I protest, remembering to whisper. "They do it in the movies all the time." I find a rock without too much trouble and wrap the note around it. I stand up, take aim and throw.

It hits the dirt in the yard with a near silent thud, narrowly missing the lid of an oil drum.

I drop behind the pile of wood, certain that somebody heard and is going to come running out. We wait. We wait some more. Nobody comes.

"Now what?" I ask, my teeth chattering worse than ever.

Eldora answers by scooting around the wood pile, walking almost to the front door and picking up our note. Back behind the wood pile, she outlines what we must do.

"We'll go right up to the door and yell help the poor. We're Halloweening just like everybody else, see. And then when somebody comes to the door, we tell them about the beer." She stops, satisfied with her plan.

168

"Just like that, we tell One Eye Klewicki to his face that his boys stole his beer!"

"Yes, just like that," Eldora says.

"Let me try to throw it again," I plead, never wanting a face-to-face meeting with One Eye.

Eldora shrugs like she knows it's not going to work. But this time the rock hits dead center, bounces off the door and whacks into the pile of cans on the porch. The clang is enough to wake the dead. Eldora and I drop flat to the ground behind the wood pile.

The door bursts open and four heads stick out. Two are front and center and two are in back. The ones in back are probably card players but I can't tell who they are. Out front is One Eye, easy to identify with his bushy red beard, bald head and gray underwear shoved up past his elbows. Gimpy McGee's there with him, wrapped in an old army coat, same as usual.

"Damn fool kids," growls Gimpy, stepping out the door and kicking the pile of cans. "Out beggin," I suppose.

"Niver git Halloween beggers out here," One Eye tells him. "Some'uns up ta somethin." He walks around to the end of the porch.

"Forget it," growls Gimpy. "Let's get back to the game." Suddenly he stops dead. "Where's my Strohs?" He grabs Klewicki by the front of his underwear and points to a spot by the front door. "My six bottles a beer is gone. Set it right thar when I come. You take my beer?" he demands.

Before I can say boo or stop her, Eldora shoots out from behind the wood pile. "That's what we wanted to tell you," she hollers. "About the beer. We saw them; we hid so they wouldn't see us but we saw them."

"Who you be?" snarls One Eye. He spits. "Whatcha think yer doin here? Get offen my prop'ty."

"The beer," breathes Eldora, almost losing her voice.

"I said git," One Eye snarls again, looking like he really means it.

"Just you wait a spell." Gimpy stops him. "I guess that's my beer they's talking about here." He turns to Eldora, and to me as I finally force myself to come out from behind the wood pile and join her. "What's this 'bout beer?"

"Klewicki boys," gasps Eldora, fear in her voice, something I've never heard before. "They grabbed the beer and ran to our fort."

"My boys!?" snarls One Eye, disbelief in his voice. "Now you git afor I make you git." .

"You just hold off here." Gimpy tells him.

"It's like we said; they grabbed the beer and ran off to our fort," Eldora says again. "We heard them talking when we were still in the woods."

"We were on our way here to come begging," I add, trying to make it sound like what we were doing at Klewicki's made some sense, which anybody in their right mind would know made no sense at all.

And I guess One Eye knows that as well: "No fool comes beggin here," he confirms my thoughts and spits by way of an exclamation point. "N you got a fort!" he snorts in disbelief.

"Fool kids carted off the old Polinski dog kennel 'n built it into a fort," Gimpy tells him. "I been watchin' em at it."

Eldora and I gulp over this, but Eldora manages to get it out one more time: "We heard them talk about taking it to our fort."

"They were going to drink it all," I chime in, hoping to add weight to a story that's beginning to sound more and more unconvincing even to me.

"Having a party," adds Eldora. "Maybe with girls."

I want to kick her before she goes on.

"I'm gettin my shotgun," says Gimpy, heading toward his place. "Teach the fools a lesson with a load a buckshot."

"Now you jest stop right there," snaps One Eye. "Nobody's goin' nowheres thout me. My boys know bettern steal beer, specially offen my porch. I'm getting' my gun." He goes inside. The two heads behind him disappear.

"Too bad we're not going to see this," Eldora whispers.

"We can get there if we run, I tell Eldora. "Give me the flashlight and I'll go first."

Eldora hands me the flashlight and we hurdle into bushes and bash ourselves against trees but we run as fast as we can. We make it to our hiding place just ahead of stomping and cursing sounds coming from the woods. The racket is followed by three men. One of the heads must have come along for the fun, I guess.

"Cain't use shotguns on kids," cautions the head, maybe coming along to ward off disaster rather than for fun.

"Can scare the crap outta em," says Gimpy.

The three are making more noise than a herd of elephants so I guess it's not going to be a surprise attack, which is too bad. I had hoped to see our fort surrounded with cries of come out before we shoot or something like that. Anyway, the roof topples off and a surprised Darrell Klewicki, clutching a bottle of beer—Stroh's, I'm hoping—stands in the glare of three flashlights. He's soon followed by his brother Clarence.

Nobody gets a chance to say a word before Gimpy charges. "A stealin' my beer," he yells, knocking the bottle out of Darrell's hand and sending him flying out of the fort and into the roots of a nearby tree.

Not to be outdone, One Eye grabs Clarence by the scruff of the neck, hauls him out of the fort like he was a plucked chicken, and drop kicks him to the ground. "Ain'tcha got any manners!" he snarls. "Stealin' someuns beer!"

"Get up, you thief," yells Gimpy, still working on Darrell, poking him with the barrel of his shotgun.

"It's the army for you two, I'm thinkin'," growls One Eye. "Yep, the army. Won't be stealin' any beer there, I betcha."

"Ya cain't put us inta the army, Paw," whines Clarence. "We ain't old nough.

"Yer as old as I say you air," snaps One Eye. "Now git home the both a ya afore I let Gimpy fill yer britches full a shot." He whacks them across the back of the head to get them on their way. "Gotta whup some sense into ya afore the army'll even want ya."

Eldora and I wait until it's been quiet long enough for us to be sure everybody's gone. Then we crawl out from behind our hiding place. We beam at one another— broad, white grins in coal-blackened faces.

Suddenly Eldora smacks me on the back: "Worst thing anybody ever did to those poor, poor Klewicki boys." Her voice is heavy with sadness before she starts to giggle.

"I suppose it is pretty sinful what we did," I admit. Then I giggle right along with her. "But it was the best sin I ever committed in my whole life!"

Exhausted and laughing all the way, Eldora and I make our way back to her house where we say good-by, but not before she hands me a sack full of most of her father's Halloween candy.

When I get home Thomas and Elizabeth are sitting at the table sorting out their Halloween candy. I can hardly wait to tell what happened. How Gimpy and One Eye yanked the Klewickis out of the fort, tossed them all over the woods and threatened them with buckshot. And how One Eye's going to put them in the army. The telling it is almost as good as the seeing it.

Finally, I choose my first piece of candy, a banana caramel. As I chew on the sweet, sticky goo I decide this Halloween was lots better than going around yelling help the poor.

Thirteen forever? Well maybe not forever
but a year or two would be nice.

20

NOVEMBER took a long time coming and going but Thanksgiving, almost stuck in the middle, was worth it. We had a chicken from Old Mrs. Lockgaar that we stuffed with bread crumbs and raisins and a black walnut cake made from the nuts we collected last fall. Cracking the shells turns your fingers black but the cake was worth it.

Winter's here now. You can't pretend it's not anymore. Snow's always on the ground and it's pitch dark when I wake up in the morning. How can it be morning when it's still night outside?

That's what I'm thinking as I pull my head out of the covers. I take a breath. Frosty clouds blow around my face. I brush away the dusting of snow on the blanket and turn over in bed.

"On the cusp of change," I mutter as a mattress spring pokes me in the back. According to Miss Olaf, that's where Europe is right now, on the cusp of change. It sounds really painful—being on the cusp of anything.

Elizabeth tells me to shut up and quit yanking at the covers.

I think about staying under the covers longer but the smell of flapjacks hot off the stove hurries me out of bed. My father came home for Thanksgiving and he's still here. He never stays long and he must be getting ready to leave again because when I get down from the attic I see he's wearing the wrinkled brown suit he always wears when he goes on the road, that and a striped railroad cap. The suit looks like maybe it lives a different life. I don't know about the railroad cap.

My father usually cooks when he's here. Every once in awhile he'll bring home a steak and cook steak and eggs, a lumberman's breakfast, he calls it. Pancakes are good, though, and I dig into them.

After breakfast I pull on snowpants, sweater, coat, scarf, hat, galoshes and the heavy mittens I found at the Goodwill last week. I stop for a minute before opening the door to the bitter cold outside.

"Hey young lady," my father calls me back. "I'm heading to Pittsburgh today, hear they're hiring at the steel mills." He pulls my cap off and messes my already messy hair. "So you be good and don't take any wooden nickels." He always says that, though I've never seen a wooden nickel.

I had hoped he would stay until Christmas. "What about Christmas?" I ask.

"Don't you worry none; I'll be back afore then."

Pittsburgh's a long way and Christmas is only a few weeks away I want to tell him. But I don't. I hurry out the door and close it fast to keep the heat inside.

As usual I head for the creek. Elizabeth walks the road with Ruth Wildebrandt, her best friend, and doesn't seem to care if the wind blows her away. I slide down the side of the creek and step on the ice to make sure it won't crack. It's slippery but holds. I stay inside as long as I can before climbing out and running to the school.

I head into the cloak room and remove my winter clothes before sitting on the floor to take off my galoshes.

"I wish yew'd go ta the party," whispers a voice in my right ear. I know right away it's Florence. The party she's talking about is the Christmas party for the older grades. It's at night, the last day of school before vacation.

Downstairs parties—kindergarten through sixth grade—are in the daytime.

"I be alone iffen yew don't go."

I doubt that, not if Fat Eddie goes, but I don't say it.

"I don't think so, Florence," I tell her, tugging on my galoshes. "Eldora and I don't like parties."

"Leery'll be there," roars a voice from over my head. Who else but Sheldon "I may bring some mistletoe," he adds, kneeling down and yanking off my galoshes. He pulls me to my feet and I can feel the heat from his freckled face on my cheeks. "Now you come, ya hear, Leery."

"Yes, pleez come, Laura," chimes in Florence.

"I'll think about it," I tell her.

"She'll be there," Sheldon says before he runs out of the clock room to the sound of the first bell.

Florence follows and I yank off my
snowpants and drop into my seat just ahead
of the second bell and Miss Olaf.

Miss Olaf, our teacher, tries hard to keep
everybody thinking Magna Charta, but it's
not working too well. The Christmas party is
on everybody's mind—now on mine as well.
I agree with Eldora how neither of us likes
parties. But now Florence is after me to go
and I'm trying to be friendly to Florence. I
don't care about Sheldon.

I guess my mind is off wandering again
because I miss seeing Fat Eddie pass a note to
Florence. But Miss Olaf, who sees everything,
catches him.

"The note," Miss Olaf demands, holding
out her hand.

Fat Eddie goes red in the face but gets up
and hands the note to Miss Olaf.

"Now, Edward," she says. "You must have
had something important you wanted to tell
Florence during our discussion of the Magna

Charta. You may feel free now to share it with the rest of the class."

I don't know what Fat Eddie wanted to tell Florence but even Miss Olaf knows it's not something he wants to share with the class. He mumbles "it was nothing, Miss Olaf." It doesn't come out too strong but I think she agrees with him, that it was nothing, because she rips up the note and drops it in the wastebasket. Then she goes back to the Magna Charta, which is a lot less interesting than wondering what was in Fat Eddie's note.

Finally after a long day of not getting much done, Miss Olaf reminds the class about the Christmas party decorations meeting in the study room after school. The information is for Rosemary and Heidi who are the only ones on the committee from our room. Rosemary is on most committees. Heidi probably just tags along.

The days go fast and Christmas comes closer and closer. Our father isn't home yet.

"I wish he'd come home," I tell Elizabeth as I work on my Christmas present for Eldora. It was going to be a lantern for our fort but now it's a lantern just for Eldora. We don't use our fort much now that the Klewicki boys found it and used it. It's spoiled somehow.

Anyway, I found this big can behind Zancowski's grocery store and decided it would make a good lantern if I poked holes in it and painted it red. Tonight I'm working on the holes, making them in the shape of stars.

"He'll be here," Elizabeth says. "He's never missed Christmas." She changes the subject: "Are you going to the Christmas party?" Elizabeth is party chairman and asks everybody that.

Before I can answer there's a loud thump on the door, followed by more thumps. It has to be Benjoe. He has ice skates hanging around his neck.

"Pond's frozen at Wildebrandt's." He stops and looks around. "So—what are you waiting for? Get your skates and let's go." Wildebrandt's pond belongs to a herd of cows in summer but in winter it belongs to us.

Edward gives me the nod, him being in charge, so I hurry and get ready.

Outside, moonlight bounces off the snow and the stars are silver in a black sky. There's no wind so the snow stays underfoot where it belongs instead of flying up into your face. Good for skating.

When we get to the pond Thomas and Benjoe drop their skates and head for the woods at the edge of the field. Thomas hollers for some help, looking right at me, so I follow. I hear him tell Benjoe that he's going to join the navy along with him.

"That's silly," I say, even though he wasn't talking to me. "You're not old enough to join the navy."

"I wasn't talking to you," he tells me, though I already knew that. He turns to Benjoe: "We'll sign up together."

Benjoe laughs: "Great idea. But we need those letters. As soon as you write mine, I'll write yours."

I don't think that's funny but before I can say anything, Thomas loads my arms up with twigs and small branches—and dozens of black widow spiders. I imagine I can feel them crawling up my arms to my neck and on to my juggler vein. I forget about the navy and hurry to the ice to drop my sticks. I hate spiders worse than anything, even mosquitoes.

Thomas and Benjoe get a fire going. Benjoe cracks jokes as they work. Elizabeth ignores him. I wonder about her as I pull on my skates. Elizabeth's usually first on the ice.

With the fire roaring, Thomas skates off. He's spotted Ruth Wildebrandt who gets a lot of his attention these days. Benjoe asks Elizabeth if she's going to skate or just sit there. She gives him a not too friendly look and he skates off. I think it's a good time for me to leave too.

I skate until somebody yells "crack the whip." To crack the whip you have to line up holding hands. The cracker, this time Thomas, skates in small circles while everybody else skates as fast as they can around and around him. When the cracker feels like it, he digs his skates into the ice and snaps the whip. That's when you go flying, especially the skater at the end. I like being on the end. Skating is easy for me, maybe because I'm so skinny.

Thomas cracks and we spin like tops before flying across the ice and into the snow piles that line the edge.

"Hey there, Lizzie Bizzie!" comes a yell from the dark. "We hear tell Mary Margaret's cookin' a bun in her oven. Has ta get hitched. Whatcha hear?"

The Klewicki boys! What are they doing here? They're supposed to be in the army. That's what One-Eye said. And what are they yelling about? Mary Margaret? In Elizabeth's class? A bun in the oven? I know what it means but I know it's not a nice thing to say.

"You just be quiet!" Elizabeth yells. "It's none of your business."

"Aw now, Lizzie, jess cause we ain't thar no more don't mean we don' ker bout skool news," says Clarence. "Ain't that right, Darrell?" he asks his brother.

Darrell laughs: "Specially Mary Margaret." They run off laughing.

After they leave, Elizabeth whacks the fire so hard sparks fly off and sizzle in the snow.

189

"What's wrong, Elizabeth?" I ask, dropping down on the log beside her. "Is it about Mary Margaret?" Lots of girls get married.

"Laura, you wouldn't understand. Mother's right about us not belonging here."

Mother's always saying how we don't belong here but here we are anyway.

Just then Ruth skates up, followed by Thomas. "Did you know about Mary Margaret?" she asks Elizabeth, sounding like she hopes the answer is no.

Elizabeth nods her head and hits the fire another blow.

"Hey, watch it!" yells Thomas.

"Elizabeth doesn't have anything against the fire," Ruth begins, "but she must have against marriage because Mary Margaret's is bothering her."

"So she's getting married—so what," Thomas says and skates off.

"I'm leaving," Elizabeth announces.

"Me, too," I say, not knowing why but thinking I should.

"Her life is over!" Elizabeth exclaims after not saying a word until we're halfway home. "Can you keep a secret?" she asks, changing whatever subject she had in mind, which must have been Mary Margaret.

I guess I can, though the only secret I can remember having is Ellen Allen's secret about her father beating up her mother. But that wasn't much of a secret because everybody in the subdivision already knew it.

"I'm going away to college," Elizabeth announces. "I'm going to be a Philadelphia lawyer."

Elizabeth's always going to be a Philadelphia lawyer so this is nothing new, but going away to college is.

"You can't go to college," I remind her. Even I know college isn't free, not like the free show out behind the school in the summer time.

"I know, silly, but I'm going anyway. In Chicago," she adds in a proud voice.

"You're leaving home!" That can't be what she means. "I don't want you to leave home."

"Of course I'm leaving home. Everybody leaves home when they go to college. You wouldn't want me to stay around here and get married the second I'm out of school, would you?" She doesn't expect an answer I can see because she goes on. "Mrs. Price is moving to Chicago. She says if I come with her she'll send me to college. I can take classes while the twins are in school."

The Prices are moving to Chicago and taking Elizabeth with them is all I can think.

"I can come home—on the train—for Christmas and a week in the summer."

On the train! I've never been on a train. "Why is it a secret?" I ask, remembering that she asked if I could keep one.

"I haven't told Mother."

"Oh," is all I say. I feel sad. I wish everything didn't have to change.

At home Elizabeth and I head up to bed. Mother won't be told anything tonight because she's working late. We don't hear her or Thomas come in.

21

WE'RE SURE it was late for Thomas when he won't get up to go to school in the morning. "I think I'm sick," he yells to Elizabeth who tells him to get out of bed.

Edward and Mother are long gone so they aren't here to make him get up. Now that Edward has a car he takes Mother to her cleaning job before he heads to the lumber yard. The two of them used to have to take two buses to get to work before he got the old Ford from Mr. Lambert.

I'm a little late myself this morning so I grab a piece of bread and spread oleo and sugar on it and run out the door.

At school it's Christmas party, Christmas party. That's all anybody talks about: who's going, who's not, who's going with who. There are some whispers about Mary Margaret but not much because in seventh grade you're not supposed to know what happened to Mary Margaret.

Florence is after me again about going to the party and Sheldon keeps telling me he knows I'll be there. Eldora shakes her head and says parties are silly. I agree with her but I'm not sure I agree about this party. After all, Elizabeth is in charge; doesn't that mean I should go? My head begins to ache and I'm glad when the last bell rings and I can go home.

Elizabeth and I are the only ones around tonight. Mother's working and Edward must be at the lumber yard. I don't know where Thomas is but he's often out with Benjoe someplace.

After Elizabeth and I share a quick dinner I finish Eldora's Christmas present. Then I go to bed. It seems to me the day has been twice as long as most others.

I'm sound asleep when loud voices wake me up: "No! No! I will not allow it!" Mother cries. "I won't let you go!"

"I'm going and you can't stop me!" Thomas yells. "Now, I'm going to bed. I have to get an early start in the morning."

"Edward," Mother pleads, her voice filled with the sound of tears. "Stop him."

I've never heard her like this. I'm afraid. "Elizabeth," I whisper, as she sits up in bed beside me. "Why are they fighting?"

Mother continues: "He's too young to be wandering the road like some bum."

"There's no one else," Thomas cries, his voice breaking. "You know that. Edward needs to keep his job; you need to work. Elizabeth can't go. There's just me."

"He's right, Ma," Edward agrees.

What are they talking about? Go where? Why? I turn to Elizabeth. "What?" I ask.

"Shhh," she cautions me. "They don't want to worry us, but I know. Father's sick in Pittsburgh—very sick. One of the passing men, you know, the ones on the road, stopped by when Thomas was home from school today."

I know these men. Sad-eyed and shabby, they show up at our door now and again. Mother says not to open the door but Thomas always does. Sometimes they have a message from our father. Mostly they ask for a potato to roast, sometimes only a drink of water.

I cover my mouth with my hands. Elizabeth puts her arms around me. "It will be all right," she says. "Thomas will find him and bring him home."

In the morning we're all up early, watchingThomas prepare to leave. He plans to hitch over to the main highway to catch a ride with one of the trucks traveling east.

197

"Promise me you'll send a postcard," Mother says. She hands him a five dollar bill telling him to put it in his shoe.

Thomas puts the address of the flophouse the man gave him in his corduroy knickers along with the clean handkerchief Mother forces on him. He puts the bill in his shoe and whistles as he pulls on jacket, knit cap, mittens and galoshes. He wants us to know how ordinary this all is. Then he's out the door.

I want to cry but I don't.

With Thomas gone the house is too quiet. And it's too big. I guess he took up more room than the rest of us. Mother quits asking me to wind up the victrola. Edward spends most evenings at the lumber yard and Elizabeth doesn't say anything, not even to tell Mother about Mrs. Price's offer. She just sits at the table doing her homework. At school Miss Olaf scolds me for not paying attention in class.

Every day after school I run to the mailbox. Before opening it I cross my fingers, close my eyes and say a prayer, not asking His will be done but mine. Every day there's nothing from Thomas.

Soon it's Tuesday, almost a week gone and still no postcard. The house is dark, no matter how many kerosene lamps I light.

Wednesday I don't want to get out of bed. I wish I had stayed there. In class we read about Alaska. Why would anybody care about Alaska—a place so cold that people sleep in ice houses? I guess I don't care because when Miss Olaf calls on me with a question, I can't answer it. She scolds me again for not paying attention: "One more time, Laura, when you are found not paying attention and you and I will have a talk after school."

"Yes, Miss Olaf," I answer. Having a talk with Miss Olaf is not something anybody ever wants to do.

After school I run home and to the mailbox. I skip the crossed fingers and prayer as they haven't done any good so far. I slam the box open hoping to smack the door into the wooden post.

A card! Smudged and wrinkled and looking like a dog chewed on it sits in the box.

"*Mother and everybody else,*" it reads in the cramped space. "*I'm here and he's sick. Took 3 hitches to get here. Got work washing dishes. Be home after awhile. He won't die or anything.*"

I shove the card in my pocket and spin like a top. I throw snow in the air until I'm covered. I flop in the deep drift by the road and swish my arms back and forth.

"It'll never fly," comes a voice I know.

It's Benjoe and he seems to always find me doing something stupid. But this time I don't care. I want to share my news. I hand him the card.

In two seconds, Thomas reads it, hands it back, whoops in the air and joins me in the ditch. He shoves snow down my back; I rub his face in it. By the time he jumps out, saying he has to go, we look like rumpled snowmen.

I hurry inside to light the lamps and build a fire. When everybody else gets home the house is bright and warm.

At dinner the victrola plays Straus and Mother hums and sings. Edward talks about Ann, Mr. Lambert's daughter and for sure his girlfriend. Elizabeth talks about the Christmas party and the dress she's going to wear. I sit at the table and smile, happy to have things back to normal.

22

THE DAY OF the Christmas party arrives. School closes at noon. The door to the study room has been shut tight for days. Half the desks from the room fill the hallways. As for the party, I finally decide to go. I guess I knew all the time I was going but didn't want to admit it.

After class Eldora meets me in the cloakroom where we plan to exchange gifts. I won't see her again until after the Christmas vacation as she's again going to Cincinnati to stay with her grandmother. Eldora seems to spend a lot of time with her grandmother.

"I hope you like this one," Eldora says as she hands me a package that I call tell is a book.

"Wait, I have something for you." I reach up over the coat rack to bring down my bulky package.

"Me first," Eldora says, shoving her round glasses up her freckled nose, something she does when she's excited.

I open Eldora's gift: *Call of the Wild* by Jack London.

"Oh, Eldora!" I yelp. "This is yours; you can't give it to me." I know it's hers because I saw it on the shelf in her bedroom.

"I know it's mine, silly. That's why I'm giving it to you."

"Oh, Eldora," is all I can say again but I guess it's enough because she hugs me and her glasses snag in my hair and we both laugh.

"How can you give it away?" I ask. I can't believe anybody would give away one of their books.

"I've read it," she says. "Besides, I like having you have it. Now, how about my present?" She holds out her hand.

"Mine's not so special," I tell her, feeling silly about what I made.

Eldora opens my package. "Oh, Laura!" She holds the lantern up so the ceiling light shines through the cut out stars. "This is extra special. It goes on top of my bookshelf with a candle in it the minute I get home."

I believe her. "I'm glad you like it," I say, cradling my new book.

"Have fun at the Christmas party, Laura," Eldora suddenly says. Then adds: "I don't hate all parties." She giggles, "Just most of them."

We pull on our winter clothes and get ready to go.

"Maybe when I graduate I'll go to my prom," Eldora tells me as we walk down the stairs. "Then again, maybe I won't." We both laugh.

I hurry home and get a blaze going in the pot-bellied stove.

Elizabeth comes in shortly after me. She wants to talk clothes—mostly my clothes—so we climb the ladder to the attic.

"You can't wear that same old dress, Laura," she tells me, as we walk up the stairs. It doesn't fit you anymore. She's talking about the red and blue print that I wore to Edward's graduation last year. It's my best dress. I like the way it flares out when I spin around. I have noticed, though, that it's getting tight in places.

"Try on my blue with the sash, the one Mrs. Price gave me last year. I bet it will fit you now." She holds it out and I try it on, knowing it won't fit. I'm so skinny nothing fits.

I put it on. "See," I tell her. We have to laugh at the way it hangs on me like I'm a clothes hanger instead of a person.

Suddenly the door downstairs bangs open. "Hey! Anybody home?"

Elizabeth and I hop down the steps, taking two at a time. Thomas and Father stand there tossing burlap bags aside and shaking snow off their heads.

We're so excited we almost fall over ourselves trying to see who can get to them first.

"Hey, hold on," Thomas yells. "There's enough of me to go around."

Father gives us both a hug and moves in to the fire. He looks pale and thin, his suit hanging on him, but his smile is big.

"Did you take any wooden nickels whilst I was gone?" he asks, mussing my hair.

"All I was given," I tell him.

We sit and talk while waiting for Mother and Edward to get home. Or Elizabeth and Father sit and talk while Thomas runs off to get Benjoe. Then the talk continue.

When Mother and Edward get home Thomas' stories are told all over again with lots of hugs and happy tears.

"I knew Thomas could do it," pipes up Benjoe, like only he could know that.

"The hitch to Pittsburgh took longer than I thought it would," Thomas says, trying to excuse himself for not writing sooner. "Then I had to find him—whew, what a flophouse—and get some grub into him before I could take time to look for a card or anything. That fiver came in handy, Ma," he adds.

"Thomas acted like a grown man the whole time," Father tells Mother. "Getting himself a job—which's more than I've been able to do—and taking good care of his old man." He gives Thomas a slap on the shoulders.

Thomas beams and looks at Mother like this should show her a grown man like him doesn't need any more schooling. "I'm thinkin' about joining the navy," he blurts out.

"Nothing wrong with the navy," Father says.

"Everything's wrong with the navy!" Mother says sharply. "You have two more years of schooling." She pauses, takes a deep breath, then continues: "But—when you finish I'll think about it. That's all I'm going to say on the subject. Thomas looks at Benjoe. They both shrug.

"It's a deal," says Thomas, like he had any other choice.

"I hate to change the subject," says Elizabeth who is doing just that, "but tonight's the school Christmas party." She looks at Thomas. "Don't you want to go?"

"Thought I'd missed it," he says. "Want to go?" he asks Benjoe.

"Benjoe's not invited," Elizabeth reminds him. "He's not in school."

"Well, I just invited him. If anybody asks, just say he's going right after Christmas."

"Is he?" questions Elizabeth.

208

"Course not," says Thomas. "Nobody goes to school who doesn't have to. He gives Mother a look that she pretends not to see.

I can drop you off at school after dinner," Edward offers. "I've got an important meeting with Ann's father tonight. He clears his throat like he has something else to say but doesn't. I wonder if it's about his job—or about Ann. Is this more change for the family?

Dinner is noisy, as usual, because everybody has something to say or a question to ask Thomas or Father.

"I'm quitting the road." Father stops the talk.

We wait. Nobody says anything.

"No factory work out there." He pauses. "But I'm a pretty good cook. Think I can get something around here slinging hash?"

Mother's eyes tear up and mine feel the same way. Everybody talks at once, trying to let him know how happy we are.

"Elizabeth also has some good news," Mother interrupts.

Elizabeth looks at me and frowns. I shake my head.

"I cleaned for Mrs. Price this week." Mother looks at Elizabeth. "Tell everybody what she told me."

Elizabeth, who I can see is relieved to know her good news isn't Mother's bad news, is happy to do as she's told. I'm happy too but am reminded again that the family won't be the same.

Time to dress for the party. I settle on an old corduroy skirt but wonder what to put on top. Then I remember the blouse I found at the Goodwill last summer. It's not a winter blouse but it has a beautiful butterfly embroidered on the collar and is perfect except for a rip down the back. I meant to fix the rip but never got around to it. Elizabeth says to wear her red sweater, that it will hide the rip and look Christmasy at the same time.

Elizabeth looks beautiful in green velvet, a dress Mrs. Price gave her.

"May I have this dance?" Father asks as we come down the steps.

Thomas and Benjoe, in honor of the party, have slicked their hair back. Thomas' brown curls won't stay slicked but Benjoe's dark hair stays exactly where he put it.

We pile into Edward's car, glad not to have to walk in the snow tonight. Edward drops us off, saying he'll be back at eleven to pick us up.

23

THE SCHOOL WINDOWS are filled with lights and we hear excited voices before we even open the door. Elizabeth and Thomas and Benjoe rush up the stairs. I hang back, not sure how I feel about being here. All of a sudden seventh grade seems too young.

I take my time climbing the stairs. In the cloakroom, I hang up my things, wondering what to do next.

"I wuz afeered yew wouldn't come, Laura," Florence whispers, coming into the cloakroom. "I been awaitin."

My eyes pop when I see her. "Florence!" I exclaim. "You look like a movie star." And she does.

"Oh, no I don't." She looks embarrassed and hangs her head. "This here dress is just somethin Ma's Harry got fer me; he got us all party rags fer Christmas."

"Florence's dress is red and green plaid of something that rustles like leaves in the wind. And her hair isn't in its usual bun but swept up in back and held in place with a comb that sparkles like Christmas lights.

"Merry Christmas," Florence suddenly whispers while I'm still admiring this once again new Florence. She hands me a package in white tissue paper tied with a red string.

A present? I feel sad. "I don't have a present for you."

"Yer my friend," Florence whispers, like that explains everything. "Open it," she urges.

I open the package. It's a bright red bow with a double tail of some kind hanging from the middle.

"Oh, look," Florence says, almost not whispering. "It just matches yer sweater."

It does, but what do I do with it. "It's a bowtie," I say.

"Oh, no," Florence giggles, a first, I think. "Let me show yew how ta wear it." She leads me to the girls' lavatory where we face the mirror over the sink.

Florence pulls my hair back and ties it with the two tails. This leaves the bow sitting square on top.

"It's so purty," exclaims Florence. "Look."

I turn sideways to see. I gasp. It is pretty. So is my hair. Instead of bushing out all over me, it's bunched in back under a bright red bow. A few small curls hang around my face. I can't believe it's me or my hair.

"Oh, Florence," I exclaim. "I like it."

214

Florence smiles in a way I've never seen before. "Let's go ter the party," she says, leading the way.

We arrive at the study room door where mostly upper grade students seem to be filling the space inside.

Where are the others who said they were coming, I wonder, again not sure I want to be here.

Florence clearly doesn't feel the same. "Mistletoe!" she exclaims, pointing to a green sprig dotted with white berries that's hanging over the door.

"Iffen yew git caught under it, yew have ter let whoiver catches yew kiss yew."

Yes, that's the rule, and a silly one. If I had anything to say about it, I'd get rid of that rule. And the mistletoe as well.

"We hafta run thru," giggles Florence, taking my hand and pulling me to the door.

This is a new giggling Florence, I can see that. But she's right; we have to run through.

We make it safely to the other side to find that nobody paid any attention to our escape. Florence looks disappointed. Not me. Who wants to be kissed, for goodness sake!

I look around the room. Christmas is every place—greens tied with red bows, cutouts of stars and snowflakes, paper wreaths and Chinese lanterns. The best, though, is the Christmas tree. It stands tall and bright in the corner with string after string of colored lights, more than I have ever seen, I think. Where did all the lights come from, I wonder? Who could own so many? We don't have lights for our tree but we don't have electricity so it would be silly for us to have lights.

Along with the lights are strings of cranberries and red and green popcorn balls. They loop over all the branches. I don't think I've ever seen a tree like it.

Elizabeth and Thomas and Benjoe stand in one corner of the room with a bunch of

216

upper class students. Heidi and Rosemary, looking like Christmas packages in red and green velvet are at the piano with Heidi's mother. I don't see Sheldon any place.

Florence giggles beside me and I hear Fat Eddie's voice. They leave together.

At the back of the room next to the Christmas tree is a small platform. Mr. Fletcher, the janitor, is up there with his fiddle and Mr. Bloomgarter, twelfth grade history teacher, has his accordion. Heidi's mother, puffed up with importance, sits at the piano where it stands beside the platform.

Miss Olaf strides to the middle of the platform. "Boys on this side of the room and girls on the other," she commands. You would know if there's any commanding to be done, Miss Olaf would be there to do it.

"No boys allowed to leave the room," she orders as there's a rush for the door by half the boys in the room.

"Hurry, hurry," she orders. "Line up. We're going to start with a Virginia reel."

Miss Olaf keeps at it until almost everybody in the room has been pushed into doing what she wants. I try to hide but she catches me.

When we're all lined up, we're told to walk forward and the person opposite us will be our partner for the dance. I walk as slowly as I can, hoping there'll be nobody left when I get there. Just when I think I've made it, Sheldon shoves himself right in front of me. He's late as usual and his hair is still wet from where he slicked it down.

The Virginia reel is a simple thing, almost not a dance at all because a boy and girl just skip through the middle of a line with boys on one side and girls on the other. At the end of the line they twirl around and the next boy and girl start skipping through. Nobody should have any trouble with a Virginia reel.

On our first twirl Sheldon and I try to go two different ways. On our second twirl, we spin until I'm so dizzy I bump into the piano. Heidi's mother frowns and makes awful noises. We don't have a third twirl.

"Aw, Leery," he tells me when the dance is over. "It's 'cause yer so small. If you were a bigger size, I couldn't spin you so fast."

Maybe he's right, I go flying a lot with crack-the-whip.

The music changes to something more like a dance. A few boys and girls try but because there are more girls willing to try, they dance together. A lot of teachers at the party dance, though, so it's nice to see what dancing is supposed to look like.

Sheldon and Fat Eddie wander off with some boys. Florence and I go to look at the punch and cookie table. The table, a long narrow one, is at the opposite end of the room from the Christmas tree and dance area. A punch bowl surrounded by evergreen branches and paper cups sits in the middle. Plates of cookies take up the rest of the table. There are gingerbread men, frosted stars and trees and candy canes, nut balls rolled in powdered sugar. I settle on a gingerbread man but it's hard to choose.

Florence and I fill paper cups with punch and sit in one of the student desks that line the walls.

"I don't much ker fer the music," Florence says. "Hit don't seem much lik what they dance to when I go ter the show."

I have to agree. It doesn't seem much like what they do in the movies.

Florence and I watch the dancers and eat cookies. Fat Eddie and Sheldon and a lot of the other boys have left the room.

Elizabeth comes by and complains: "It's those magazines that Mr. Fletcher keeps in the furnace room. It's disgusting."

Mr. Fletcher's magazines seem a big attraction.

Elizabeth must have sent somebody to bring the boys back because after awhile they begin to slink into the party room. I don't see anybody run to catch them under the mistletoe.

Sheldon and Fat Eddie return. Sheldon goes to get some punch asking if I want some. I shake my head and he heads for the bowl.

Finally Miss Olaf announces it's the last dance and she's going to make it girls' choice because that's the only way to get the boys out onto the floor.

All the girls giggle. All the boys look red in the face. They don't want to dance but they don't want to not be asked either. I see Elizabeth with some tall, skinny boy from twelfth grade. Hilda and Thomas head out together. A lot of couples go out this time.

"I know you wanted to ask me to dance."

Benjoe!

Sheldon frowns.

"I didn't ask you to dance," I tell Benjoe. "Besides, I thought you were still in the furnace room."

"And what do you know about the furnace room?," he asks.

I turn red in the face.

He laughs. "I've seen all those magazines." He pulls me to my feet. "Come on, Laura, since you asked me. Let's go."

"I didn't ask you," I tell him again. "And I can't dance."

"She didn't ask you," Sheldon says. Benjoe ignores him.

"Oh yes you can," Benjoe tells me. "I saw your ma teach you."

Benjoe saw my mother pull the victrola outside and give us dance lessons in the front yard! But it doesn't matter. I still can't dance. The only music we have is Straus and nobody dances to that that I can see.

"This is easy," says Benjoe. "Just like Mother said."

My face turns even redder but I let him take me out with the other dancers.

"Here we go," Benjoe says, pulling me along to the music.

And we dance. I mean Benjoe dances and I dance and we do it together, at the same time. My feet go where his feet go and his feet go where mine go and they don't step on each other getting there. It's like doing Viennese only not with my mother.

We finish and Benjoe laughs. "Aren't you glad you asked me?" He heads off to Thomas and Hilda who have finished dancing if you can call what they were doing dancing. I wonder where Benjoe learned to dance. Somehow I don't think it was from watching my mother.

Sheldon moves in close behind me, still wearing a frown.

Suddenly the overhead lights go out and the room is dark except for the Christmas tree. Hushed sighs and oohs and ahhs fill the room.

"Let us end the evening with *Silent Night*," Miss Olaf says.

"Leery," Sheldon whispers. "Something's over your head."

Mistletoe! I feel it resting on my head.

Then, almost in the middle of the silent and the holy night, Sheldon turns me around and kisses me. He slides his lips down my forehead, over my nose, and onto my mouth. His lips feel like butterfly wings. My stomach feels like a bunch of birds are nesting in it. Not awful nesting, just a lot of fluttering around. Is this what a kiss does to you?

My face burns and I'm glad the lights are out. When they come on, I look around, hoping nobody noticed.

Miss Olaf calls out: "Merry Christmas to everyone." Then she adds: "Don't forget the cleanup committee meets here at ten in the morning."

I glance down and see Sheldon's hand. "That's not mistletoe!" I yell.

"What?" Sheldon says. "It's not?" He holds a sprig of evergreen up in the air. He examines it from every angle. "Are you sure?" he asks. There's a big smile on his face and snickers from a few students near us.

"You tricked me!" I tell him, quieter this time.

He laughs: "Oh, Leery, tricking you is half the fun."

I should be mad, or at least act mad, but it's hard to with Sheldon. He's always just being Sheldon.

"Don't be mad, Leery," he says. "It was for fun."

I guess I can't be mad at anybody tonight.

"Time to go, Laura," Elizabeth calls out, already in her coat. "Edward's out front. Get your clothes."

I hurry to the cloakroom, followed closely by Sheldon.

"Will you go skating with me some time," he asks as I pull on my things. "Tomorrow night?" he adds.

"I can't skate at night unless somebody in my family comes along," I tell him.

He laughs: "You can bring them all as long as you come, Leery." He reaches in his pocket. "Merry Christmas," he says, handing me a small, flat box.

"Oh, Sheldon." I don't know what to say. I can't say I don't have a gift for him because even if I had one, which I don't, I couldn't give it to him. Girls don't give boys gifts, for goodness sake.

"Open it," Sheldon says.

"Laura, you better come down right now," Elizabeth calls up the stairs.

"Go on," Sheldon urges. "Open it."

I open the box. It's a white, folded handkerchief with a ribbon across the top and a pink letter L embroidered in one corner.

"L for Laura," I say. "It's so pretty."

"L for Leery," Sheldon corrects me. He laughs.

For some reason I can't help but laugh right along with him.

"Laura, you come down right now or walk home," Thomas yells up the stairs.

"I'm coming; I'm coming," I yell back and run for the stairs.

"Tomorrow night at the pond," Sheldon says, following me. "Ice skating, remember."

"Tomorrow night," I promise.

Outside in the snow, Sheldon laughs and howls a few times before he leaps in the air and heads off.

He always does that.

I run to Edward's car and squeeze in the middle in the back.

"So, what's with the big guy?" Thomas asks. "The one who kept you upstairs so long?"

"I think Laura—or is it Leery——'s got a boyfriend," chimes in Benjoe. "And we all better watch out because he's a big guy."

"Oh, stop," scolds Elizabeth. "Quit teasing Laura."

"*On the first day of Christmas,*" Edward sings as we drive away. "My *truelove gave to me.*"

"A *partridge in a pear tree,*" Elizabeth follows.

"*On the second day of Christmas my truelove gave to me,*" Edward continues.

"*Two turtledoves,*" sings Thomas, his turn.

"And *a partridge in a pear tree,*" sings Elizabeth.

The next one is mine: "*Three French hens.*"

"*Two turtle doves,*" sings Thomas.

"And *a partridge in a pear tree,*" sings Elizabeth.

Benjoe's turn is the colling birds, whatever a colling bird is.

We sing until nobody can remember what comes next. Then the fun begins where we make up gifts. By the time we finish, we're home.

As we get out of the car I can't help but think how perfect the night was. "I wish everything could stay just the way it is," I whisper. "I don't want anything to change, ever."

Elizabeth hears me: "Don't be silly," she says. "Do you want to be thirteen forever?"

Thirteen forever? Well, maybe not forever, but a year or two would be nice. I giggle, thinking about it.

Elizabeth opens the door, letting pale yellow light spill out onto the snow. We go inside.

ABOUT THE AUTHOR

Joan Schmeichel is the author of the coming of age series *The Times of Laura Grey* and *More Times of Laura Grey*, as well as *Dey Calls Me Maggie,* a time travel historical novel for young teens. Under the name Joan Roth she has also written a number of stories and poems for curriculum materials. The first chapter in *The Times of Laura Grey* was originally published by the Traverse City Writers Press as the 2011 fiction winner titled *Kisses for Laura.* Joan is also the author of the play: *Is It Raining in Poughkeepsie?* If Joan isn't writing, she is either on the golf course or working on Kakuro puzzles. Joan and her husband Neill have lived most of their lives in Michigan, most of the time in Ann Arbor or Jackson, with a few years in the Philadelphia area. After their retirement they settled into their vacation home in Kewadin, Michigan.

More Books by Joan Schmeichel

It's a Doggone Life

Dey Calls Me Maggie

More Times of Laura Grey

All are available at Amazon

Printed in Great Britain
by Amazon